'This is what [...] **for.' His voice** [...] **of primitive desire.**

Pride and desire surged through him, fighting for supremacy. In a few months' time this woman was going to give him the greatest prize any man could wish for. He had proved that his magnificent body combined libido with potency—and she was the living proof of it. This moment deserved something special.

The darkness had been pushed back a little by the soft glow of dimmed lights. He drank in her naked beauty. Their first couplings had taken place under the dark veil of night. Now there was no hiding from him. She cried out and tried to cover herself with her hands. Then she saw the effect that her body was having on him. She looked up into his face, her eyes full of eloquence.

'I want to see the body that is going to give me my son,' he told her.

Christina Hollis was born in Somerset, and now lives in the idyllic Wye valley. She was born reading, and her childhood dream was to become a writer. This was realised when she became a successful journalist and lecturer in organic horticulture. Then she gave it all up to become a full-time mother of two and to run half an acre of productive country garden. Writing Mills & Boon® romances is another ambition realised. It fills most of her time, between complicated rural school runs. The rest of her life is divided between garden and kitchen, either growing fruit and vegetables or cooking with them. Her daughter's cat always closely supervises everything she does around the home, from typing to picking strawberries!

Recent titles by the same author:

THE ITALIAN BILLIONAIRE'S VIRGIN

COUNT GIOVANNI'S VIRGIN

BY
CHRISTINA HOLLIS

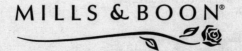

MILLS & BOON®

All the characters in this book have no existence outside the imagination of the author, and have no relation whatsoever to anyone bearing the same name or names. They are not even distantly inspired by any individual known or unknown to the author, and all the incidents are pure invention.

First published in Great Britain 2007
Harlequin Mills & Boon Limited,
Eton House, 18-24 Paradise Road, Richmond, Surrey TW9 1SR

© Christina Hollis 2007

ISBN-13: 978 0 263 85337 7

Set in Times Roman 10½ on 12¾ pt
01-0707-52440

Printed and bound in Spain
by Litografia Rosés, S.A., Barcelona

COUNT GIOVANNI'S VIRGIN

To Martyn, who makes all things possible.

CHAPTER ONE

KATIE had expected Tuscany to be hot and dusty. She had not expected it to be so beautiful, and perfumed with the scent of herbs basking under a hard blue sky.

'You will be expected to hit the ground running, Miss Carter. Signor Amato rarely makes allowances for anyone—especially not an interior designer!' Plump, neatly suited Eduardo leaned forward and tapped on the glass separating them from the limousine's chauffeur. He issued a curt order in Italian and then settled back into the cream leather seat beside her. 'Signor Amato must visit his city office later this morning and he is attending a dinner given by an Australian delegation this evening. His day operates to the second. As his right-hand man at the Villa Antico, I must ensure that we reach there on time.'

'I'm sorry my flight was cancelled. I was supposed to land yesterday.' Katie's fingers gripped her briefcase. Of all the days to get caught up in a security alert. This dream job was really important to her. Giovanni Amato had a reputation as the world's most reclusive billionaire. When the Marchesa di San Marco's personal recommendation had secured Katie the job of restyling his ancestral home north of Florence, she had hardly been able to believe her luck. Everything had been planned down to the last detail. She had arranged to stay overnight in Milan, to make sure she was fresh for this morning meeting. Then all her arrangements had collapsed like a house of cards. Instead of being cool, calm and collected, Katie was stiff and overtired after a night spent in the airport. Her palms were suspiciously damp and her heart was racing, too. This was not how she was supposed to arrive on her first day in heaven.

Working in a place like this will be no hardship at all, she thought as they sped through rolling countryside dotted with pretty little stone and tile villages. Eventually the sleek black Amato limousine turned in at an enormous pair of wrought iron gates. The chauffeur lowered his window and checked in to security. Obediently the gates slid open. Then the car set off down a long avenue of lime trees. Katie gasped as a classic Tuscan villa loomed into view. It was only slightly smaller than Windsor Castle.

An intense young man in Armani emerged from the house as the car drew up. He opened Katie's door before the vehicle stopped, breaking into its air-conditioned comfort. The heat enveloped Katie like a thermal blanket.

'My goodness, what lovely weather,' she began, but Antico staff were not chosen for their small talk.

'Signor Amato will see you in the White Office, Miss Carter,' the butler said to Katie, then turned to Eduardo. 'She is late.'

'Show me the way and I'll run,' said Katie.

Giovanni Amato was standing with his back to the door. Windows stretched from floor to ceiling in his cathedral-like office and silhouetted his tall, muscular frame. From that first moment, Katie knew he would be a force to be reckoned with. A commanding figure in beautifully cut linen trousers and a crisp white shirt, he made a gesture of acknowledgement as she entered the room. Then he went back to pouring a flow of eloquent Italian into the tiny mobile at his ear. Katie had to wait until he finished his call before she got her first proper look at him.

'I hope I did not disturb you, Signor Amato,' she said as he turned, then stopped. He had a face that men could fear but women could not resist. One look into those intense grey eyes and she might have been lost—but for his expression. Momentarily it looked as though he had the weight of the world on his shoulders. And then the handsome, regular features broke into a practised smile.

'Not at all—it's Miss Carter, isn't it? I'm pleasantly surprised to meet you. The contractors Mima usually recommends are tough Neapolitans!' he said in perfect English. Raising one hand, he ran fingers through his thick dark hair. There was no need. It was cut short enough to remain tidy without attention, but that did not stop him. He flexed his shoulders, and the cut of his shirt hinted at powerful muscles beneath. Then, stretching his left arm with lazy elegance he inspected the silver Rolex on his wrist.

'I was told you would be late, but five minutes? That is nothing.' He smiled again and for a moment there was an air of devilment about him. 'Sometimes my staff worry too much, but I am not about to criticise them. When they are working well, my days run smoothly. That is all I ask.'

Katie was speechless. He was absolutely charming and his easy manner continued as he walked around his work-station and perched on the edge, facing her.

'A desk puts up such a barrier between people, don't you think?' Reaching behind him, he picked up a china *Viola* mug, tasted the contents and pulled a face. 'Cold cappuccino retains all of its caffeine but none of its pleasure. Excuse me while I ring for a replacement.'

Katie looked around the spacious office as he rang down to his kitchens. The Villa Antico's faded splendour was obvious here. All Giovanni Amato's high-tech equipment had been plonked in the centre of a gracious room full of peeling paintwork and threadbare carpets.

'The kitchens have bad news, I am afraid, Miss Carter. I am supposed to leave in ten minutes for a meeting in Milan and my super-efficient PA suggests we don't linger over coffee.' He laughed, shaking his head.

'Er…yes—ok…' Katie floundered. This man was as serious as he was good-looking. There was clearly a time limit to this audience with him. 'Right, well, I'm Katie Carter…'

'I know. You come with the highest recommendations from my friend the Marchesa di San Marco. I don't know how much she has told you, but I inherited this place from my father a while ago. When he was in residence it was allowed to decline into the pitiful condition you see all around you. Now I have decided it is time for the Villa Antico to rise again. I want to restore the high standards of the past, so all traces of its most recent occupancy are to be swept away. With no time to restyle it myself, I need a specialist. All my staff here work to the highest standards. Contractors are expected to have the same attitude.' He was lost in thought for a moment and then his lips flickered a spark of amusement at her. 'Do you know, I've just realised that in some small way I envy you, Miss Carter. Here you are—a self-made woman, Mima tells me, who has fought her way up from nowhere. You are responsible only for yourself. It makes me wonder how far I could have taken Amato International if I had started from scratch. Family loyalty and tradition are my driving forces, and there's no doubt I have the killer instinct necessary to protect the old firm, but what are the qualities you needed to start from nothing, I wonder?'

He gazed at her appreciatively for some moments, a half smile playing around his lips. Katie could only guess how devastating its full power might be, but his expression soon became serious again.

'The fact is that I need a base where I can retire from public life, Miss Carter. I don't intend to entertain here—that takes place on my yacht or in one of my city apartments. But when Mima visited, she was so full of the wonders you had worked at her Villa Adriatica she thought you would be good for this old place. I have never yet disappointed a lady and I was not about to begin with Mima. So here you are.' He spread his hands in a gesture of welcome.

Katie said nothing. She knew that clients always had strong ideas about what they wanted. She expected such a successful, busy man to have a list of requirements. She waited for him to reel them off. Instead, his smile remained immovable. He could have the most beautiful eyes in the world, Katie thought, if it wasn't for one thing. They were dove-grey, long-lashed and perfect—but there was a hint of something dark behind them. What was it, she wondered—pain? Suspicion? The way he shifted slightly when he mentioned his father hinted at some sort of friction in his past. There were secrets beneath all that easy, designer-dressed efficiency. Katie could sense it.

Their exchange was interrupted by the arrival of Eduardo, with a message that it was time to leave. Launching himself from the table edge, Giovanni pulled his jacket from its hanger in a cupboard and slung it over his shoulder.

'I am due in Milan, Miss Carter. Do you know the Amato building? They serve the most *excellent* refreshments there.' He turned to his PA. 'The young lady and I will continue our meeting on the flight, Eduardo. As we go downstairs we will be passing one of the first areas for improvement, Miss Carter.

It has not been redecorated for at least thirty years, to my certain knowledge.'

He held the door open for her and they passed from the office into a warren of halls and wood-panelled passages. Katie was awestruck at the size and splendour of the place. It would take her a lifetime to find her way about. She was booked to be here for only thirty days. At the end of the long passageway, Giovanni seized the polished brass handles of a pair of double doors. As he opened them, a gust of warm air hit them. It was perfumed with beeswax polish. Katie followed him into a vast room. Shafts of sunlight from tall windows fell across ancient floorboards that centuries of polishing had given a rich golden glow.

'When you need to find this place again, it is called the Smoking Gallery,' he said, answering one of her questions before she could ask it.

'Then you are a smoker, Signor Amato?'

He chuckled. 'No. My great-grandfather saw some interesting architecture while visiting England a century ago. When he returned, he ordered his men to recreate some chimneys of the type he had seen there. Unfortunately, because they do not draw smoke upwards from the fire, it always blows back down.'

He walked over to a great black marble fireplace on one side of the room. Positioning one foot carefully on the fender, he pointed up at the chimney-breast. Ancient wooden panels hung there, illustrating the Amato family tree. It was decorated with brightly coloured coats of arms and ancestral flags and descended from the ceiling like a many-fingered stalactite. Names were picked out in gold leaf. Beside each one was either a shield or a banner, enamelled with the appropriate family colours.

This man had history. Katie wondered what it was. She glanced at him and was about to speak, but found his face bleak and pained. This look was replaced almost instantly with his usual charming smile. Despite that, Katie was alarmed. She looked back at the panelling to try and see what had made his expression slip.

His family tree was nothing but facts and figures. A huge span of Amato history was laid out before her. It trickled down to end on one side with the single golden name Giovanni Francisco Salvatore Amato. Her magnificent surroundings nudged Katie into a conclusion. This man had no wife and no offspring—yet. That must be what concerns him, she thought. There might be advantages in being born a commoner, like her, after all. Giovanni Amato must shoulder the sole responsibility of continuing his grand family line.

Katie soon discovered it was dangerous to make any assumptions about her new employer. They were not couriered to the city by private jet. Instead, a helicopter stood on the estate's private airfield, ready to go. After helping her in, he swung himself into the pilot's seat and clipped on a headset.

'I'm surprised billionaires don't make business come to them, rather than the other way around,' Katie managed to say, despite her initial terror. He did not reply immediately, but they lifted off smoothly enough. Then he steered the machine around to give her a swallow's eye view of the Villa Antico.

'There are two reasons why I do this, Miss Carter.' He hovered, reversed, and then worked a dignified slalom around his rooftops. The helicopter was so low, Katie could have looked right down inside its barley sugar chimneys—if she had not been clinging to her seat and fighting to keep her nerve.

'The first reason is that, no matter how good the satellite link, nothing replaces a handshake. People like to meet me in person. And who am I to deny them that pleasure?' With the twitch of an eyebrow, he shot a playful look straight at her heart. It scored a direct hit. The effect was obvious, but Katie knew she had to hide it. Women must turn to jelly before him all the time, and she never followed the herd.

He side-slipped the helicopter speedily to the north-west.

'Does that gasp mean you want me to slow down, Miss Carter?' With a reassuring smile he checked and levelled the machine. 'Don't worry. I've never lost a passenger yet.'

Relieved, Katie released her death-grip on the upholstery.

'You said there were *two* reasons, Signor Amato.'

He looked at her with a grin of pure relish.

'Oh, yes…' Making an impossibly tight turn, he dropped the helicopter again to sweep a down-draught along his venerable avenue of lime trees. 'The second reason is that I enjoy it, Miss Carter.'

Katie soon overcame her initial fear of helicopter travel. In time, she even managed to glance out sideways. Looking down was still too much of a challenge. She wondered what her mother would make of this. Poor mousy little Katie, who hated any sort of fuss, had grown up to travel in a billionaire's private helicopter!

Her wonder increased as they drew near Milan. Instead of cypress trees, city skyscrapers rose above a layer of wispy cloud.

'See that? It is the headquarters of Amato International.' Giovanni pointed out a building. As they flew closer, Katie saw a white H on its roof. She gripped her seat, nervous again as Giovanni dropped in towards it.

'It began as a local concern, centuries ago,' he told her when they had landed safely. 'Then my family was approached by merchants who were looking for investment. Things improved rapidly after that. Early in the last century, car makers had to decide how to fuel their engines. Investors were faced with a similar choice.'

'Amato International chose to support petrol?' Katie said and her host laughed in agreement. His family must have been blessed with good luck a million times over the generations, Katie thought as she followed him into the executive lift. She wondered if he appreciated it. Despite his affable nature, she guessed that Signor Giovanni Amato kept his real thoughts well and truly hidden.

They travelled to the executive suite in a lift lined with mirrored glass. Katie found it hard to know where to look— or rather, she knew exactly where to look but tried to resist. Giovanni Amato was reflected all around her. If she kept her eyes to the front, it was impossible to avoid his acute stare. His tall figure flanked her on either side—one real, one reflected. Looking up was no escape from his presence either, although it was not so nerve racking.

They stepped out of the lift into ankle-deep carpet. Katie automatically priced the wall-to-wall luxury at not less than one hundred euros per square metre. The fact that she did such a thing brought her up short. Perhaps work really was invading her whole life if she had started putting a cost on her surroundings.

Katie had seen for herself that family life and work did not mix. Her past made her determined to lead a quiet life. Work was the thing. She could please people simply by doing something that she loved. That was her recipe for a happy life so far and it was making her very successful. She had started a Saturday job in her local fabric shop at the age of fourteen. It had been intended as a few hours' escape from home each week, but from the moment she had walked in on her first day

Katie had been in paradise. Colours and textures entranced her. From rich ruby velvets to star-spangled chiffons, the fabric shop had provided a release from the dull reality of keeping house. Katie's dream of a career in interior design had led to a college course. Then she had set up her own consultancy business. Now here she was, working with some of the richest and most influential people in the world. Even now she could hardly believe her luck!

Such a privilege had its price. Katie had a reputation for complete discretion. She said nothing, no matter what. She had seen and heard things that would make her a fortune many times over if she revealed them to the press. But, in Katie's opinion, money was not everything. She knew what she was worth and charged no more and no less than that. When it came to giving service and satisfaction to a client, she was streets ahead. Her favourite quotation was, 'It's never crowded when you go the extra mile.' Word soon spread. She had been able to take on assistants to share the workload. Yet Katie still did all the most important things alone. She had seen what happened when you got too closely involved with other people.

She was not going to let anyone ruin *her* life.

The executive lounge was wall-to-wall excess. Garish modern art jostled for attention around the red-painted walls. One side of the room was entirely made of glass. Like an eagle's nest it gave the executives of Amato International a regal view of the city, far below. There were a lot of puzzled looks and the odd smirk as Katie walked nervously into the office with Giovanni Amato. Instinctively she kept a step or two behind him and tried to be invisible. He was having none of it. Putting a protective hand to her shoulder, he drew her forward and made a direct announcement to the leering of paunchy officials.

'Gentlemen, Miss Carter is head of a firm of contractors. They will be refurbishing my Villa Antico, so she needs to get an idea of my tastes. I may have many skills, but I lack the time to discover if decorating is one of them. I have brought her here to use you, and these offices, as some examples of what I do *not* need in my private life,' he teased them affably, and they responded to him with laughter.

'Miss Carter will be working closely with me over the next month and needs to get a taste of my methods and working conditions.' He continued, 'To save time, I have brought her here to meet the secretaries.'

The executives of Amato International were still grinning, but now they looked good-natured, not feral. In their world, women were either slaves or honorary men. Katie let Giovanni lead her past them, grateful she was wearing practical working clothes. Her black trouser suit was severe almost to the point of being funereal, but she still had to run an off-putting gamut of appreciative stares from the other executives.

Giovanni Amato did not share his male executives' hobby of ogling. Katie decided it was probably because he knew how it felt to be openly admired. When he led her into a large anteroom staffed by personal assistants and secretaries, there was a flurry of excitement. Every woman in the place stopped to look at him. He seemed not to notice, cheerfully introducing Katie as his new contractor and then going back to join his colleagues. She was left to field a thousand questions. All the girls were desperate to know what it was like inside the Villa Antico. Some had attended a staff party held in its grounds during the previous summer, but none had entered the actual buildings. Katie explained that so far she had only seen the White Office.

'Be sure to let us know what the bedrooms are like, won't

you?' winked Signora Gabo. She was a greying, matronly type—but it hadn't stopped her blushing and giggling with the rest of them when Giovanni Amato had walked in. 'Every A-list woman from the glossy magazines wants an invitation to his house, but nobody seems to be having much luck.'

Felicia, a thin girl peering through curtains of long blonde hair extensions, nodded sagely. 'All the society hostesses are trying to get in on the act. I've heard him talking to my boss Guido about it—everyone wants to introduce the world's most eligible bachelor to the love of his life. He's getting a bit tired of it, he says. The trouble is, there are so few women of quality for him to choose from. Of course, a man like that can't marry just anybody.'

'Why not?' Katie's innocence met with peals of laughter.

'Because he's a count, that's why! Though he doesn't use his title when he's working. The girl Gorgeous Giovanni marries will come from one of the titled houses of Europe, I expect—although going by that poem made up by a newspaper columnist to describe some of them, he'd be better off choosing one of us: "Four feet two, eyes of blue, twenty stone and not a clue…"'

'That's a terrible thing to write!' Katie gasped, but she had to suppress a guilty giggle. 'Didn't anybody complain?'

'No—mind you, I doubt if many of them can read.' Signora Gabo looked over the top of her glasses as she tapped sheets of paper into a neat pile. 'That isn't what aristocratic women are for, Katie.'

'He wants a titled virgin with an IQ larger than her bust, apparently,' Felicia chipped in. 'We all want him to get married soon. There's nothing like a wedding!' She sighed, and everyone else joined in. 'But it doesn't look as though we're going to be in luck. He trawls through shoals of celeb-

rity women who all think they might become his next
Contessa, but he's always careful not to linger too long over
any one girl.'

Signora Gabo shook her head. 'He works too hard for that.
Hanging on to an inheritance is difficult. He makes it look
easy, but only because he puts his good family name before
everything else. We have his father, the old count, to thank for
making him like that. Signor Giovanni has to increase the
value of what can be passed on to his heirs, and that takes a
lot of doing,' she finished with a wise nod.

'He won't have anyone to leave it to if he doesn't father a
child himself,' Katie replied.

She could not wait to get back to the villa and start planning
her work. Going to Milan with Giovanni had given her plenty
of time to discover his dislikes and priorities. It had also shown
her the pace at which he worked, and the pressure. When they
left Milan behind and headed back to the Villa Antico, his relief
was visible. Katie almost felt relaxed about the return flight.

'I had a useful time at your office, Signor Amato. Although
I did find your fellow executives a bit overwhelming.'

'They are good men, but their brains are in their trousers
when it comes to beautiful women.'

Katie blushed at the compliment and found it almost impossible to look at him.

There were no acrobatics on the way home. Giovanni set
his helicopter down in its circle with pinpoint accuracy. Then
he went to help her from the cockpit. This time Katie hesitated before taking his hand. If he noticed anything at all, it
was the delay. He reached out to support her wrist with a firm,
sure grip. Katie felt her stomach contract, but she was irresis-
tibly drawn out of her seat.

In desperation she tried to keep focused on her work.

'This trip was extremely valuable in getting a taste of your working conditions, Signor Amato. But it was rather taken up by talking to your staff.'

'And lunch.' He slipped her a wicked glance. 'I gather the girls showed you the best trattoria in Milan?'

Katie blushed again, conscious of the way his life revolved around his working day. 'We were all back exactly on time, Signor. I wonder—would it be possible for me to attend Amato International again at some point and perhaps take a look around the rest of your office block?'

'Why not come straight out and say that you'd like a contract to rework *all* my property, Miss Carter?' An enigmatic smile hovered around his lips. 'You have a lot of ambition for one so young, no?'

Katie coloured again, but this time she kept her nerve. 'Yes. I can't deny that the idea was in the back of my mind. But nothing more than that.'

'Good thinking—having an eye to the future is invaluable in business,' he agreed, to Katie's relief. They were crossing a stretch of grass that separated his airstrip from the villa. He stopped and reached up to pull off his tie and unfasten the top two buttons of his shirt. A tantalising glimpse of dark hair became visible, below his throat. It made Katie wonder what else his austere white shirt was hiding. Amazed at such an unusual thought, she sucked in a breath of wonder. Then she heard a soft laugh and looked up.

'My, my, Miss Carter, that is a blush as chaste as any Contessa. The Marchesa di San Marco never told me you had noble blood in your veins when she recommended your work. I hope you aren't one of her grasping relatives, down on their luck.'

It was spoken lightly, but it still brought Katie up short. She could hardly believe anyone could make such an accusation in so offhand a manner. Fighting off gold-diggers was one thing, but Giovanni Amato should not be allowed to get away with insulting his workers.

'I am nobody's grasping relative! I got this job on my own merits,' she responded fiercely. She would show him—he would have to come down off his high horse when he discovered what a good worker she was.

'And so I should hope,' Giovanni replied with satisfaction. 'I don't have the time to supervise your every movement while you are here.'

'I would not let you.' Katie tilted her chin and looked him straight in the eyes, then wished she hadn't. He *was* gorgeous. There was no other word for it.

'Excellent. I'm glad we agree,' he said evenly. And, with a gesture for her to follow, he strolled off towards his house.

CHAPTER TWO

'THIS is Signor Amato's itinerary for the next thirty days.' Eduardo handed Katie a piece of heavy cream paper that bore the Amato crest. 'Business appointments are in red, social ones in green, and engagements combining the two are cross-hatched. The timing of your month here was chosen because he will be based at the Villa Antico, rather than travelling between his other properties here in Italy and abroad. You will be able to experience Signor Amato's taste for yourself and, of course, talk to him about his personal preferences.'

'My goodness,' Katie murmured as she studied a closely typed timetable. It covered the current month in detail, but the previous and following weeks also crowded in at the top and bottom of his busy schedule in note form. 'The Hamptons, Manhattan, a yacht, Nice… Does the man never spend more than a couple of nights in any of these places?'

'No.' Eduardo looked thoughtful and then reached out a neatly manicured hand for the paper she held. 'I understand from Signor Amato that you are to be allowed full access to the villa, in which case now might be an ideal moment to make a study of the White Bedroom. Signor Amato is guest of honour at a dinner this evening. If you begin now, Miss Carter, you will have some time in which to work upstairs, undisturbed.'

'Oh, but I couldn't possibly go to Signor Amato's suite now. He'll be getting ready to go out.'

Eduardo laughed, his prosperous jowls shimmering. 'I do not mean you should work on his personal suite, Miss Carter. You would be dealing with separate rooms. They were used, until the old Count's death, for—' he looked up, searching for what to say among the carved fruit and flowers that decorated the ceiling of his office '—something that Signor Amato would rather have wiped from the record as soon as possible, shall we say?'

Katie's imagination went into overdrive, but she was too discreet to ask for more details. This impressed Giovanni's assistant, who soon lost his initial suspicion of her. He led her through the marble halls quite cheerfully, but was surprised when she wanted to be shown her own suite first. 'I shan't be a minute, Eduardo, but I need to collect a toolbox... Wow!' she gasped as he showed her into a large salon.

On closer inspection it was as faded and shabby as the rest of the house, but Katie's first impression was of glamour, space and light. It was a world away from her small city flat. All the huge windows had been thrown open to air her suite, and filmy net curtains billowed in a sweetly scented breeze coming in from the gardens. Work forgotten, Katie wandered through her spacious temporary home. She gasped at the marble, gold and mirrors of her bathroom and marvelled at the size of her dressing room. She had brought the minimum amount of luggage and her first thought was that it would be lost in the echoing vastness of cupboards and racks when she came to unpack. Then she opened a closet door and found that her things had already been put away, and the suitcases stored on their own stands. Katie decided that if this was how the other half lived, she could get used to it quite easily. She made a mental note to thank whoever had dealt with her things later, but for now there was work to be done.

'I offer a complete interior design service, Eduardo,' she said as he queried the kit she had picked up from her room. 'There is no point in covering up infested timber or unsafe structure. Naturally, mine is only an initial survey. I employ a qualified structural engineer to provide the definitive report. But as a first move I like to find out what is going on for myself.' She did not tell Eduardo the real reason for her curiosity. Before she'd teamed up with Marcus, her tame surveyor, several sub-contractors had tried to take advantage of her. They'd thought a young woman would neither know nor care if they skimped on their work. Katie had taught them otherwise. She was not willing to compromise. Everyone employed by Carter Interiors had to give one hundred per cent all the time—and no excuses. That included her, too.

Eduardo carried an enormous keyring. It jangled under the weight of the crudest ironware Katie had seen. Some of the keys must have dated back to a time when the first parts of the ancient villa had been built. After a dizzying number of right and left turns, they entered a strangely silent corridor. All sounds of domestic staff going about their work died away. A strip of Indian carpet laid on the polished boards muffled sound. Faded flock wallpaper covered the walls. The ceiling must have been three metres high and the corridor a couple of metres wide at least, but after the great open spaces of the rest of the villa it felt almost cramped. Its chocolate-brown paintwork and burnt sienna wall-covering only added to the feeling of being enclosed. Katie had to fight the impulse to duck her head. They passed several gleaming panelled doors. Then Eduardo stopped at one and inserted a well-worn brass key in its lock. The door opened. The room beyond was white—white walls, white paintwork and white muslin curtains. In its centre stood an enormous white circular bed, the size of a Roman arena.

'Here we are, Miss Carter. What do you think? Seductive, eh?' Eduardo could not hide the sarcasm in his voice.

'It's extremely…bright, isn't it?'

'Not at night, Miss Carter. I can assure you of that.'

'That beautiful old fireplace over there—does it still work?'

'Sadly no, miss. This salon is immediately above the Smoking Gallery. The rooms share a chimney.'

'That is a pity.' Katie frowned. She was already making a note to contact an expert in open fires. Something had to be done to make this room more welcoming. The place must be made less clinical and more of a—Katie flinched at the word—boudoir. It was the last effect she wanted to create for a truly masculine man like Giovanni Amato, but there might be a middle way. If there were, she would find it.

'Thank you, Eduardo,' she said as the PA moved to leave. 'Will it be all right if I visit the gallery below, later?'

'You are to be given free access to the villa, Miss Carter. Signor Amato is not expected to return from his evening out until the early hours. Although I expect you will be finished long before then.'

It only felt like ten minutes later when Eduardo returned with a silver tray bearing coffee and treats.

'Signor Amato has just left for dinner, miss. He suggested that you might like some refreshments. And what are your own arrangements this evening?'

'Am I supposed to be going out, too?'

'It is not obligatory, miss.' Eduardo smiled. 'You may order dinner to be served in your room, in the dining hall or, if you would prefer to send out for a pizza, we can do that for you.'

Katie hoped her face did not show how impressed she was. Staying here was sheer luxury—and she was being paid for it, too!

'What is on your menu this evening, Eduardo?' she asked politely.

His expression became almost patronising. 'Anything you desire, Miss Carter.'

Katie gasped at that. The kitchens were probably geared up to serve teeny-tiny portions of exotic food and she suddenly realised she was starving. There was another problem, too. Katie did not want to take advantage of her situation by choosing anything overly expensive. On the other hand, ordering a great pile of the bread and cheese she loved might offend her client's highly trained staff.

'In that case, I think a little chicken and salad will do nicely.' She smiled, hoping her meal would come with a slab of focaccia.

'Thank you, Miss Carter. And where would you like to eat it?'

'In my room, I think, Eduardo,' Katie decided. 'And whenever it is ready will be fine by me.'

Confusion ran over Eduardo's face. 'No, Miss Carter, that is not how this house works. We serve at the times and in the places you specify.'

Katie sat back on her heels. In other grand households she had always eaten with the staff. No one, neither Katie nor her clients, had thought to suggest anything else.

'I shall be working here for about another hour, Eduardo. When I have finished, there's something I want to check in the Smoking Gallery and then I shall retire to my suite, thank you.'

When Eduardo left, Katie allowed herself a small smile.
There are advantages to being employed by a pampered single
man, she thought.

She investigated the hospitality tray Eduardo had brought.
Six handmade biscuits sat on a china plate. The one thing
worse than being served a tiny dinner would be leaving some
of it because I've filled up on biscotti, Katie thought. After
eating two, she left the others untouched, but it was with deep
regret. Then, on impulse, she popped a couple into her
pocket—just in case dinner turned out to be fashionable
rather than filling.

By the time she carried her toolbox down to the Smoking
Gallery it was already dusk. The door was still unlocked, so
she went straight in.

A bat flickered through the enormous room, disappearing
up into the shadows. Katie shivered, relieved that it would
only take her a few moments to check her client's armorial
colours. She ran over to the fireplace. Its tall mantelpiece
meant that Giovanni Amato's entry was almost too high for
her to see through the gloom. Taking out her pocket torch, she
played it across the painted panels to pick out his name. The
beam soon fixed on the name she was looking for, but as it
did Katie noticed something else. She moved her light slightly
to the right. There was some discoloration in the wood that
had not shown up when it had been bathed in sunlight earlier
in the day. The more she looked, the more Katie saw.

Giovanni Amato's name was picked out in gold leaf, like
all the others. The difference was in the surface upon which
it had been written.

She stared. This family tree had been carefully altered,
with her client's sole name replacing two linked entries.

* * *

Katie could not sleep that night. Her mind was racing, and
there were several reasons. The sheer majesty of this beautiful place was almost overwhelming. Her rooms—which
Eduardo dismissed as 'the small guest suite'—were large,
beautiful and airy. It was difficult to stop wandering around
their threadbare luxury. Her mind was forever running over
ideas for the places she had surveyed today, but every so often
her thoughts returned to the mystery of the amended family
tree. What, or rather who, had been covered up and replaced
by Giovanni Amato's name?

For a long time she lay in bed, staring up at the shadowy
sweet chestnut beams criss-crossing her ceiling. Then she
must have fallen asleep, for suddenly she was catapulted
awake by a sound from outside. Dragging on her dressing
gown, she dashed to the elegant French windows of her
bedroom. Opening them let in a cacophony of birdsong—and
the rhythmic beat of a swimmer. Katie stepped out onto her
balcony. The Tuscan dawn engulfed her, almost as though she
had plunged into a pool herself. The early morning was still.
Its air was cool, thin and bubbling with birds. Below her, a
rectangle of water glowed with lights set below its surface.
Long, lean lines ran through it with a glass-cutter's accuracy.
Giovanni Amato was making them.

Katie took a step forward. She put her hands on the
ironwork balustrade. It was cold with condensation, but she
hardly noticed. The sight below absorbed her whole attention.
The swimming pool must be twenty metres long. Time and
again Giovanni's lithe naked body vanished in a perfect turn
at each end. Katie watched, transfixed. To the east clouds
split with sunshine, like a ripe fig. Had he only just returned
from that private dinner? She went on watching, mesmerised
by him and the thought of his punishing work schedule.

According to the list Eduardo had given her, Giovanni break-fasted at six o'clock each morning. Then he retired to work in his home office.

'Good morning, Miss Carter.'

She jumped. He had flipped out of his latest turn and was leaning back against the side of the pool. Arms outstretched along the poolside, water swirled around the rippling image of his golden body. Katie clapped her hands over her face.

'Oh, my goodness! I am so sorry, Signor Amato.'

She heard a turbulence of water and then a full-throated chuckle.

'You can uncover your eyes now, Miss Carter.'

His voice, rich with amusement, came from directly below her. She dropped her hands and looked down. He had secured a snowy white towel around his waist and was using a second one to rub his head and upper body dry. As she had suspected, he rippled with muscles. As he worked the towel, biceps and triceps flexed in a way that was impossible to ignore. Tossing it aside, he ran his fingers through the tousled thatch of his thick dark hair. Then he planted his hands on his hips and looked up at her.

'I always like to put in a hundred lengths or so before breakfast.'

'Oh, then you haven't just returned from your evening out?'

He gave an eloquent shrug. 'No—I got back a few hours ago. Sleep is not something that troubles me much.'

'I didn't have much trouble with it myself last night.' Katie gave a sigh, but it was not on account of her sleepless night. She had never seen anything like Giovanni's muscular torso. His sleek, sun-bronzed body was perfectly accentuated by a dark pelt of body hair. It shaded his chest and ran in a narrow line down his flat, toned belly. Katie tingled with nervous excitement. Until now, the only place she had seen a naked man was on TV. Now Giovanni Amato was live and loveable, right in front of her. How would it feel to run her hands over that perfect aristocratic form? The sight of him aroused her and the novelty of this new sensation increased its effect. Katie's home life and money worries did not leave much time for distractions. Temptation had always passed her by. Now she was looking straight at it.

Her eyes reached his face. Did he know what she was thinking? His expression was not giving anything away.

'I'm sorry to hear that. Did something keep you awake, Miss Carter?'

Katie's mind dragged itself away from his body and back to thoughts of the wall panel in the Smoking Gallery.

'Yes,' she said, and then thought better of bringing the subject up straight away. 'I was so full of ideas for your…White Bedroom,' she said carefully. 'I found it hard to drop off.'

'Then we must discuss your thoughts. I am eager to get that place cleaned up as soon as possible. Breakfast will be coffee and rolls. Is that OK for you?'

'It sounds wonderful.' Katie nodded.

'Good—we'll meet in the dining hall, then, in ten minutes.'

With that, he disappeared into a vine-covered pool house. Katie continued to watch for a minute or two, transfixed by what she had seen. Giovanni's body was as honed as his mind. Yet again she caught herself wondering how it would feel, and blushed.

Twenty minutes of increasingly frantic search later, Katie was desperate for a glimpse of Giovanni Amato's fully clothed body, let alone anything more interesting. She could not find the dining hall. Eventually she heard the creak of floorboards in a distant cross-passage and ran towards it. Pink-faced and panting, she caught sight of a figure just as it disappeared around a corner.

'Excuse me! I'm looking for the dining hall.'

In the silence that followed, Katie had a terrifying image of wandering the passages for the rest of her life, slowly starving to death... Then she felt a rush of relief as a young butler answered her call. 'You won't find either of them up *here*, Miss Carter.' He stared at her, mystified. 'In any case, do you mean the summer dining hall or the winter dining hall?'

Katie almost screamed with frustration, but it wasn't the boy's fault that she was lost. 'I need to be in the room where Signor Amato is taking breakfast,' she said as reasonably as panic would allow.

'Ah, that is the summer dining hall. Go back along this corridor, take the second on the right and go down two flights to the Lesser Entrance. You'll see a door in the far corner. Beyond that is the rear corridor: go straight along it and into the kitchen block. From there, the third green door to your left opens straight into the summer dining room.'

'Isn't there a short cut?' she asked desperately.

He looked her up and down. Katie's smart business suit was clearly giving him pause for thought.

'Only for those willing to take the staff lift.'

'Oh, I don't mind that. Thank you!' Katie gasped, and he led her to a hidden utility area.

Half a lifetime later she burst into a huge, echoing room of chandeliers and gilded mirrors.

'Ah, Miss Carter.' Giovanni dropped his copy of *La Repubblica* to watch her hurry to the table. 'Where is the fire? Coffee is on offer, although I feel I should recommend tea to calm your nerves.'

'I—I got lost.' Pulling back a Regency-striped chair, she took her place at the polished mahogany dining table. Giovanni had his elbows on the arms of his carver. His fingers were loosely laced before him. He made no move to show her where the drinks were, so she stood up again. In doing so, she almost collided with a butler. He had arrived silently at her elbow, teapot in hand.

'This is such an enormous house. I went around and around in circles.'

'As an interiors expert, perhaps you should not be telling me that.' Giovanni tried not to laugh, but failed. 'We shall get you a map, Miss Carter.'

His scrutiny continued as she settled herself. It was direct, but there was a certain amount of warmth behind it. Katie found it impossible to look away, despite the unsettling effect he was having on her. It was unusual enough to take break- fast with an employer, but this one seemed genuinely inter- ested in what she did for a living. It was a concern she wanted to foster, not spoil. Now she was smouldering like embers with the shame of messing up right at the beginning of her first full day. It was not a good start.

'I can only offer you my apologies, Signor Amato. It will not happen again.'

He made a sound that Katie took to be approval, but then stood up with obvious regret. 'I intended to discuss your initial plans as we ate. Unfortunately, I am due a conference call, which must be taken in my office. I'm sorry we missed this opportunity, but perhaps we can talk when I finish my own work this evening? But now I must go. Enjoy yourself. *Ciao!*'

As he left, Katie kept her head down over her cup of

Darjeeling. She was not about to head for the buffet table while there was the smallest risk she might cannon into him. That would be the *end*.

The trill of a mobile phone spoiled her plan. She heard him stop right behind her, swear softly, then answer it.

Katie sipped her tea. She was starving. How much longer would it be before she could get up from her seat without the risk of making a fool of herself in front of him? The huge dining room was so quiet it was impossible not to be aware of the stream of muffled words pouring from his phone. Eventually, Giovanni interrupted them with such honeyed thanks that Katie could not help but look around at him. The amusement she saw in his eyes made her shiver. His expression came alive and danced with her heart. She was sorry when the call ended and his expression changed. He snapped his mobile shut and popped it into his pocket again.

'I may not need to delay your beauty sleep this evening after all, Miss Carter.' He laughed and with alarm Katie felt the warm glow of his personality reach out and envelope her again. 'The fact is, I was due to be entertained by a client later today. Unfortunately my host has had to drop out. As lunch reservations at Il Ritiro are highly prized, he has kindly offered me his booking. How would you feel about coming, too? It will give me the perfect opportunity to show you some of our famous hospitality, and study your plans at the same time.'

Before Katie could reply, Giovanni was summoned to the expected conference call in his office. She let out her breath in a long sigh of relief. She had been scared that being late for breakfast might be a sacking offence. Instead, all she had lost was some time alone with him, and now she was being offered a luxury lunch to make up for it. She could have hugged herself. How lucky could one woman be?

CHAPTER THREE

KATIE worked in the Smoking Gallery all morning. While she was there, a sketch map of the Villa Antico was delivered to her. It was accompanied by a request from Giovanni that she should be at the front doors by midday. An expansive hand had added the words 'To help you find the way' and signed it with the single word 'Amato.' Determined not to be late a second time, she set the alarm on her mobile. She loved her work so much it was easy to lose track of time.

The great house was silent as she went to keep their appointment. Her own suite was bright and sunny, but a cool breeze rippled around the villa's marble halls and chestnut panelled corridors. Katie knew that it took a small army to keep the place neat and tidy. She had met most of them, and liked them. They all got on together. It was such a pity their happy group couldn't dispel the unloved feeling of this old place.

It was exactly one minute to twelve when Katie arrived at the front doors. She did not get a chance to try her strength on the great iron ring of its handle. A butler arrived as she was putting out her hand and opened the door for her. Stepping back smartly, he let in a gust of warm, herb-scented air. The courtyard faced north. Some of the large gravelled area immediately outside the house was in deep shade, but beyond its shadows the stones glowed with sun.

Giovanni was precisely on time. His Ferrari swung around from the rear of some outbuildings and stopped right beside her. Getting out of the driver's seat, he made his way around to open the passenger door. Although his smile was only formal, Katie's heart still flipped. Her usual severe black working uniform had been replaced with dark linen trousers and a pale yellow blouse and she wore strappy leather wedges to keep her feet cool, but he had the power to make it all feel hot and constricting. She had to remind herself that this was nothing more than another business meeting for a busy Italian count. It felt a lot more enticing to her.

'You look lovely, Miss Carter. It is a pleasure to see you looking a little more relaxed.' His lips twitched in a teasing smile. 'Now you are dressed to enjoy our climate.'

Katie's eyes widened. His remarks were so personal. She hadn't thought he would take much notice of what she wore, let alone expect such a compliment. In agitation she fumbled with her case of designs and, as she did so, dropped her sunglasses. While she struggled to keep hold of her slippery files, Giovanni bent and retrieved them.

'Versace?' He smiled. 'Somebody has obviously been paying you too much, Miss Carter.'

Katie cursed her clumsiness. Giovanni Amato was good-looking enough already. Now he was adding a roguish smile to his charm, which released a strange fluttering feeling within her. This was not what she wanted to experience during a business lunch. She liked things to be kept strictly impersonal, and had to throw off his gaze before answering. 'I receive what I am worth, Signor Amato.'

She heard him chuckle as he dropped into the driving seat

beside her. It was such an evocative sound that a warm rush of anticipation instantly flooded through her. She quashed it almost as swiftly. Working for this man should be exciting enough. She could do without the added surge of attraction she felt for him. Opening the car window, she tried to cool down by thinking of other things.

'You should make the air-conditioning work for you, Miss Carter,' he said as the Ferrari sped up through the hills like a bead of mercury.

'I like the perfume of this countryside.'

'It is the vines. At this time of year they are growing so quickly you can see them move.' He was smiling as he drove, resting one hand on the steering wheel, the other on the gear lever. Katie could not answer. She was trying to concentrate on the view and hoped his typically Italian driving would not send them plunging down into the river far below.

'What is the matter?'

He was looking at her, not at the narrow twisting road. Katie could not suppress a tiny noise of alarm.

'Miss Carter?'

'It's nothing. Nothing,' she strained through pursed lips.

Suddenly they were whipping around a corner at such speed she squealed like a rabbit.

'There *is* something wrong.'

Katie was almost speechless with fright. 'No—no, only…why do you drive so fast, Signor Amato?'

'Fast?' He sounded puzzled and looked down to check the dials on his dashboard. 'Oh…I should have remembered from our trip to Milan that you like to take things steadily, Miss Carter.'

He eased off the accelerator. Their speed dropped smoothly away and Katie let out her breath in a relieved stream.

'I take my driving for granted, having travelled these roads so often and for so long. It's funny that no one else has ever mentioned it to me, though.' He shot her a curious glance. Katie recognised it from their first encounter in his office. He had been fascinated then by the qualities she needed to succeed. She knew that criticising a client's skills should not be among them.

'Perhaps you would have been happier if we had come out on the company bicycles, Miss Carter?'

His words instantly punctured her worries and she laughed. '*You*? You're not telling me *you* can ride a bicycle?'

'Certainly! The Villa Antico and the countryside around it was my refuge when I was growing up. Of course, my great-uncle was in residence as count here, then.' He was now concentrating on the speedometer more than the scenery and Katie felt herself beginning to relax. Then he unconsciously turned up her thermostat again. 'I used to power up and down these hills on my trusty Tommasini. It was exhilarating.'

Katie remembered the sight of him naked in the pool. And then envisaged his strong thighs working hard as he cycled through the hills. She gave a self-conscious giggle and he laughed in return.

'That's better. You should loosen up more often, Miss Carter. Let a little of our southern warmth thaw your chilly northern efficiency.'

By the time he pulled up in the restaurant car park, Katie was almost at ease with his presence, although the thought of lunch with a billionaire was still pretty nerve-racking. She was glad when he retrieved her work from the back of the Ferrari and then opened the passenger door for her like any ordinary gentleman.

The restaurant had been created out of an ancient farmhouse. Cultivating rich guests was easier than fighting with the thin, stony soil. Katie was enchanted. There could not have been a more perfect setting among the blue Tuscan hills. To complement the picture, some tables were set outside, beneath a rose and vine draped loggia.

The head waiter came out in person to greet them.

'Ah, Signor Amato—what a pleasure it is to see you here again so soon.' The waiter clapped his hands and passed a practised eye over the case in Katie's hands. 'Will you be requiring Internet access?'

'No, not today, thank you, Luigi,' Giovanni said, and they were shown to a table beneath the twining greenery. It had the best position by far, with a spectacular view of the valley below.

Their settings were laid as they approached. Two young waiters dressed in black uniforms with crisp white aprons worked at lighting speed. They set out silver cutlery and crystal-ware, which glittered in the dappled, dancing sunlight. A covered jug of mineral water clinking with ice completed the scene.

The head waiter pulled out a delicate ironwork chair for Katie. As she took her place he picked up the intricately folded napkin on her side plate. Flicking it out with a crack, he swept it across her lap. As she thanked him, one of the other waiters handed her a menu.

Studying the copperplate handwriting before her, Katie realised she was way out of her depth. Her Italian was not good enough to choose from this list. It gave her few clues about what to expect. What if she chose something she did not like? Keeping her mind on business when faced with this gorgeous client would be difficult enough. The embarrassment of making a wrong choice of food would be too much to bear. She stared at the descriptions, desperately trying to recognise more words or phrases.

'Are you ready to order, Miss Carter?'

To confess would make her feel a fool. Instead, she fastened on something else about the list that worried her. 'There are no prices on my menu, Signor Amato.'

'That is so you can select without being distracted by the cost,' he said airily. 'Does anything particularly catch your eye?'

Katie dithered. It was all probably wonderful—and expensive. Every working-class instinct was telling her to choose the cheapest thing, which was impossible without prices. Every fibre of her self-made being begged her to go for steak. At least she could translate that, but would it seem extravagant, compared to everything else? She kept trying to decipher other descriptions. What would her host think, when someone employed to make decisions about his home couldn't choose between items on a menu?

'Is there anything you would like me to translate for you, Miss Carter?' He had thrown her a lifeline, but before she could confess he started laughing. 'Although I'm afraid my descriptions might be hazy. The staff here have been trying to teach me the correct culinary terms for years, but I'm afraid all their signature dishes still look like stew to me.'

Relieved, Katie asked him to translate the small but impressive choice of local seasonal dishes for her. In the end, she narrowed her choice down to marinated pigeon or Valdichiana beef.

'Then…may I suggest the beef?' His words were slow, gauging her reaction. 'It is my particular favourite, but don't let that influence you in *any* way.'

Katie's response to his mischievous smile made him snap his menu shut and hand it to the waiter. His order included two steaks with vegetables and a single glass of Sassicaia. As her own menu was lifted from her hands, Katie suddenly thought of something, but decided to keep quiet. Giovanni picked up on it straight away.

'Why are you looking like that, Miss Carter? You aren't having second thoughts, are you?' he queried, pouring them each a glass of water.

'I was wondering why there weren't more vegetarian options.'

'Why? You aren't a vegetarian.' He chuckled.

The casual way he dismissed her query annoyed Katie. It was too much like her mother's refusal to take anyone else's feelings into account.

'How do you know I'm not?' she countered, but instantly regretted it. There was no place in Giovanni Amato's world for nut cutlets. Where he came from, it was all haute cuisine and fine wines, she realised. *That must be why Eduardo gave me the option of a takeaway pizza last night. The villa staff probably think I don't know any better.*

Giovanni stopped laughing and looked at her. It was a rare woman who answered him back, but today he chose to take it as a good sign. Several times that morning she had taken on the doe-eyed look women always got when he was being himself. At least Miss Katie Carter had some spirit. That would make it easier when it came to stifling any romantic ambitions she might have. His heart had been out of bounds for years and he had no intention of releasing it, although she was becoming a strong temptation…

'As your host, Miss Carter, I make it my business to find out these things. For example, I happen to know that you had chicken for dinner last night. It follows, surely, that you can have no objection to eating meat,' he finished evenly. 'Now, are you going to open your file so we can start work, or have you already written me off as hopelessly controlling and manipulative?'

Katie laughed, but he did not. Although his voice was light, dark clouds were gathering in his grey eyes. The physical longing that rippled through her each time she looked at him instantly melted into concern. He is hurting, Katie thought with sudden realisation. She squashed the thought almost immediately. It was ridiculous. This man was a count, a successful businessman *and* wealthy beyond the scope of her imagination. What did he have to look downcast about? As far as she knew, the only worry in his mind would be finding a sufficiently regal mother for his future son and heir.

Other men would kill for a problem like that.

'Yes, I think we'd better get on, don't you?' she said briskly. Work would protect her from dangerous fantasies about what might be going on inside his head. This was a business meeting, pure and simple, she told herself. The sort of thing he does a dozen times a day with a dozen different people. I'm nothing special.

Unzipping her case, she brought out the first page of sketches and ideas. Immediately his attention fastened on the papers in her hand.

'Ah, this must be my father's entertainment suite…I shall certainly be glad to see that go.' He took the sheet from her with long, strong fingers and studied her work intently.

'I have contacted an expert in London,' Katie explained, 'who thinks it may be possible to modify your chimneys so that the suite and the Smoking Gallery beneath it can have open fires again. Your city offices look so modern and industrial. I thought you would like to return home to a more intimate atmosphere. That is why the new paintwork and walls have been given natural tones of cream, pale apricot and terracotta. There is still white muslin at the windows, but the rooms have been given a warmer, more relaxed feel.'

'Yes,' he said, lost in thought as he took a sip of water. 'I want a complete change, and this is an excellent start. I suppose your cosy chats with the staff have informed you that the main reason for all that white was apparently practical?'

It was Katie's turn to query him with a glance. In response he replaced his glass, put his elbows on the table and gave her a provocative look. 'Then my staff are even more discreet that I thought. Allegedly, the White Bedroom makes it easier when playing Find the Lady in the dark, Miss Carter.'

Katie felt a furious blush rising all the way up from her breasts to her face. His eyes locked with hers. He threatened to smile. Using all her self-control, Katie managed not to look away. The thought of being alone in that stateroom, in the dark, with Giovanni Amato suddenly filled her whole being. With immense effort, she fought against her feelings of anticipation. What was happening to her? This was a job of work—the one thing in life that never let her down. She had no time for dreams—even if she was sitting opposite the world's most desirable man. He is just a client, she thought fiercely. Giovanni Amato is no different from any other man.

But he was. Those intense grey eyes drilled into her like diamonds. It was as though he could see right inside her mind.

Their antipasti arrived. It was bruschetta cut into tiny shapes, each with a different topping: a rasher of salami, red beads of sun-dried tomato or slivers of fig and prosciutto twisted into intricate curls.

'You seemed a little uneasy earlier on, Miss Carter,' he enquired as they ate.

'Uneasy? No, Signor, it was simply the novelty of these lovely surroundings. I don't usually have time for restaurant lunches or a social life. I always eat at home, with my dad,'

Katie said, beginning to relax. Shaded from the sun, their table was ideal. The warmth was wonderful and the food was even better. 'Work is my life, Signor Amato.'

Giovanni nodded in approval. 'It is a shame more women do not share your dedication,' he said as one of the waiters brought out a glass of red wine on a silver salver. 'That is for my guest, thank you, Carlo.'

'I assumed it was for you,' Katie said in amazement as the Sassicaia was placed beside her. The rich red liquid glowed like stained glass in the filtered sunlight.

'I *never* drink and drive, you will be glad to learn.' He treated her to a meaningful smile.

'It was very rude of me to criticize your driving,' Katie acknowledged. 'I'm sorry.'

He waved her apology away. 'Don't mention it. It has been five years since I let anything get in the way of common sense. It is never worth it.' His last words were dark with meaning. Katie glanced up. He was gazing into the middle distance, his lips a grim line. Once more his whole expression was pained. It was so unbearable Katie felt she had to bring him back to the present. Her glass of wine provided an excuse for her to stir and break his mood. He returned to reality when he saw her take a sip. Putting the glass down again, she touched the napkin to her lips.

'Then you agree with my initial colour scheme and ideas, Signor Amato?' she said once she had his attention again. 'Of course, you need only make final decisions when you have seen samples and fabric swatches.'

'Yes, go with those ideas. I can modify them later, if necessary.' He was back to business as quick as a flash.

'Initially, I wondered about using the colours of your family crest for decorating that room,' Katie began casually as their main course arrived. He looked pleased at the quality of his beef and she decided this might be the moment to bring up the mystery that had been puzzling her. Heart thundering, she picked up her knife and fork. 'I happened to go into the Smoking Gallery at dusk to check the details. The funniest thing showed up in my torch beam. There must be a flaw in the wood of the panelling. A patch of discoloration beneath your name makes it look as though—'

'It is a flaw, most certainly.' He cut through her words as easily as he sliced his steak. Katie might have believed him, but for one thing. He was not looking at her as he spoke. Giovanni Amato's direct stare when speaking was one of the most challenging things about him. Now he refused to even glance in her direction. Katie was intrigued, but she knew better than to press the point.

'In the end, Signor, I decided that red, blue and green weren't the world's most seductive colours.'

Katie noticed him smile at her words. When he raised his head those even white teeth flashed briefly.

'Did Eduardo tell you it was my father's favourite suite?'

'He hinted at it, although without giving details, thank goodness. Your mention of what went on in there confirmed my suspicions.'

Giovanni found her reaction highly amusing. 'And so you have designed a room in which you would like to be seduced?'

Katie's eyes flew to his. It might have been meant as a joke, but when he saw her expression he stopped laughing. For the longest second in recorded time they stared at each other. Her heart turned somersaults in the turbulence of his gaze. There was definitely something hidden behind his eyes, and a sudden mad impulse made her want to reach out and touch him. She resisted. Katie was beginning to learn that when it came to Giovanni Amato, some things should remain unspoken.

She always tried not to repeat her mistakes. Next morning she arrived in the great summer dining hall well before six a.m. Giovanni was already seated at the head of the table. Dressed in a formal dark suit and pale blue shirt, he was engrossed in the business section of *La Repubblica*. As the heels of her sandals clicked across the marble floor, he put down his paper.

'*Buon giorno,* Miss Carter.' He watched as she chose a place halfway down the twenty-seat table. Today the guarded look in his eyes had been replaced by curiosity.

Katie felt bound to say something. 'Thank you for inviting me to eat breakfast with you, Signor Amato.'

He laughed off the compliment. 'Nonsense, Miss Carter, it is nothing but common courtesy. You are a guest in my house.'

Katie smiled at the butler who had arrived magically at her side. 'Not exactly, Signor. I am employed here to do a job of work. That makes me a member of your staff.'

'I don't think so. My staff don't normally wear colours and styles like that.' He raised his eyebrows at her pink, close-fitting top.

'I know, I know.' Katie blushed, as amused as he was. 'It's the effect of all this sunshine. After what you said yesterday about my working clothes, I decided to choose something more exotic than my usual starchy white shirt. I didn't think anyone would notice such a small thing. Don't worry—I'll change straight after breakfast. This top doesn't really say "work" to me, either,' she added apologetically.

Giovanni found himself unexpectedly aroused. He wondered how long it would take to work up a physical immunity to her. If she had any more nipple-skimming

T-shirts like that one among her off-duty clothes, the answer was: quite a while. He shook out the pages of his newspaper again to distract himself from his thoughts of Katie Carter and that delicious little top.

But, as Katie was served with rolls and a cappuccino, he looked up and watched her smile in thanks. She turned and caught his gaze and an unexpected spark of tension simmered between them.

She was saved from the lingering intensity of his stare by the sound of her mobile.

'Oh…' She unclipped the handset from her belt but, before she could redirect the call, Giovanni stopped her.

'Answer it, Miss Carter. I know how it is—a missed call means missed business.'

Amazed at his tolerance, Katie took her call.

'Dad. Hi—listen, it's great to hear from you, but actually I'm in a meeting at the moment—' She stopped. Her host was gesturing at her.

'Family matters are more important than business, Miss Carter. Carry on with your conversation.'

'But I can always spare a few minutes for you, Dad.' She laughed with her father as he remembered the time difference. He had thought Katie would still be getting ready for work. Her laughter soon died when she realised why he had telephoned. Giovanni lowered his newspaper completely as he saw her frown.

'Is something the matter at home, Miss Carter?' he enquired as her call ended and she clipped the mobile back on to her belt.

'Yes—and no, Signor. My mother has announced that she wants to pay an extended visit to my father. The problem is…'

She hesitated. How could she tell this virtual stranger about the walking collection of character faults that had given birth to her? Oh, if only her father wasn't so gentle and forgiving! Katie could not bear to think of him being hurt again, as he surely would be. 'The problem is that my mother rarely contacts him without some…hidden agenda. My father had heart bypass surgery not long ago, and he shouldn't be expected to take her in. I know from painful experience that her return always means trouble.'

'Your father must develop enough backbone to resist her. His recent health problems may have helped. Facing disaster often causes men to stiffen their resolve—especially when it comes to women.' Giovanni flourished his newspaper and returned to studying his stocks.

Katie seethed. His family life might have been as bad as hers, but she was not about to have her father scorned as well as her mother. Dad *is* too soft for his own good and I *am* only a guest here, but I'm not going to let him get away with that, she thought angrily.

'How can you say that, Signor Amato?'

'My own experience does not lie, Miss Carter. Unless and until the good influence of motherhood takes over, women often deceive, flatter and scheme to get their own way,' he concluded in a low voice.

Katie shook her head slowly. For his character sketch to be accurate, her mother must have been a regular Jezebel before maternity hit her. Joyce Carter's fickle, flighty behaviour had made Katie the woman she was. When puzzled, Katie always asked herself what her mother would do in similar circumstances. Then she took care to do exactly the opposite.

'Not all women are alike, Signor. Some of us are hardworking, trustworthy and loyal.'

'Hmm…' he began, and then looked thoughtful. 'I must

admit your attitude to work impresses me. I have never known any other woman put in similar hours to mine.'

'Then you must be mixing with the wrong sort of girl, Signor.'

'Whereas you don't have time to mix with men at all?'

Giovanni's statement echoed what she had hinted the day before. Work gave her no time. She had admitted that. But still she met his retort with a cool gaze. 'I have never yet met a man who understands why I feel as I do about my work. But, unlike you, Signor, I would never write off fifty per cent of the human race without first giving them a chance.'

Two dark, impenetrable expressions met across the polished mahogany of the dining table. They each reached for their coffee in the same instant, and the moment was broken.

'Where will you be working today, Miss Carter?'

'I shall continue with the first floor suites, Signor. Would you like to be present when I begin on your rooms?'

He flicked another glance at her, but found that her words had been without flirtation. The blush that lowered her long dark lashes now was one of guilt at saying the wrong thing, not coquetry. He continued to look at her long after coming to that conclusion. Something stopped him looking away.

'No. I don't think that will be necessary, Miss Carter,' he said at last.

Katie finished her light breakfast quickly. She told herself she was keen to get on with her work. This was not entirely true. Part of her wanted to escape from Giovanni Amato. Whenever she was in his presence, her body simmered. Everything about him—the drift of his aftershave, his low, confidential tone, the clear golden skin—drew her eyes to him with an urgency that could not be denied.

Early that morning, she had woken seconds before the

splash that announced his dive into the pool. Incapable of re-
sisting the lure, Katie had left her bed and gone to the French
windows. They had been left standing open all night. Katie
liked to think there was only a veil of white muslin between
her and the nightingales singing in the olive groves below.
This morning, though, her mind had been on other things.
She had not gone onto the balcony. Instead, she stayed
hidden in her room, looking out over the pool. Giovanni
Amato's naked body was perfectly illuminated by the under-
water lighting. She watched as he powered up and down,
sleek as a seal. When at last the pounding beat of his strokes
stopped and the water grew still, her heart sank. The glow
of excitement low in her stomach became an ache of longing
which had been tormenting her ever since. The only cure for
that was work—and work that avoided Giovanni Amato as
much as possible.

Keeping away from him was easier said than done. Katie
worked methodically through the first storey of the house.
After beginning with the old 'entertainment suite,' she thought
it logical to continue her work on the same floor. Unfortunately for her hormone levels, that eventually meant
entering Giovanni's office.

The White Office revolved around his enormous island of
a desk. With its banks of telephones, scanner, fax, computer
and modem links, it drew Katie's eyes almost as much as the
man behind the monolith. For nearly an hour she measured
and sketched, making notes and trying to avoid catching his
eye. In turn, he issued instructions down the phone, rattled
away at one keyboard or another and carefully ignored her.

    When her survey was over, Katie tried to tell herself she
was glad. It was not true. The atmosphere of his office fizzed.

It was the excitement of seeing and hearing a man at the top of his game, directing multi-million dollar deals worldwide.

She took a while packing the toolbox with her tape measure, pencils and notebooks. During all that time he never spoke to her. In fact he only looked up to acknowledge his PA, when Eduardo entered the office.

'*Scusi*, Signor—Miss Carter.' Eduardo nodded towards Katie as she knelt on the floor surrounded by her work. 'The Princess Miadora's office rang. Sadly, she is indisposed and will not be able to attend your party this evening after all.'

Giovanni threw down his fountain pen and clasped his hands behind his head. 'Damn. That leaves you with a planning problem, then, doesn't it, Eduardo? Who is to sit with Signor Balzone and sweet-talk him into helping the project?'

'I was hoping you might suggest a suitable replacement, Signor.'

Katie heard her client sigh. He must have shaken his head, too, because, as she picked up her things and set off for the door, Eduardo began to reel off a list of names. Katie tried not to listen, but it was impossible not to—and wonder. The Amato contacts were so starry, his address book must glow in the dark.

'The Duchess?'

'No—she told me herself she was booked solid.'

'The Marchesa Chiara?'

'She is on her yacht, somewhere in the Indian Ocean.'

'Lady Carina Foakes?'

'She's in London for her son's birthday.'

'Mrs Delabole?'

'She is off prospecting in The Hamptons, along with Myra Haigh-Davies, Kiki Lipton and all the other trust-fund talent you have tried to foist on me over the years, Eduardo.'

As Katie reached the door there was a pause in the list of eligible females. With a twinge of disappointment she realised that was the last bit of gossip she would hear.

And then Eduardo followed her out of the White Office and caught up with her as she walked along the corridor to the next suite.

'May I trouble you for a moment, Miss Carter?'

'Of course you can, Eduardo. What is it?'

'Signor Amato was wondering…' the PA began, looking shifty. Then he giggled. 'All right—to be honest, *I* was wondering…do you have any engagements this evening, Miss Carter?'

Despite his grin, Eduardo looked a worried man. Katie could not bear to heighten his tension by inventing a social life for herself.

'Er… no. Why?'

'Signor Amato is hosting a party in aid of charity on his yacht tonight. I carefully crafted the guest list months in advance, as usual, but now we find ourselves one lady short. Signor Amato's guest of honour is a single man. He cannot possibly be left without a lady to escort into dinner. I was wondering…might you agree to make up the numbers?'

Katie considered this, but not for long. Anyone would be mad to turn down the chance of mingling with the rich and famous on a billionaire's yacht.

'All right,' she said cautiously, trying to ignore the fact that she must be their guest of last resort. 'Yes—I'll do it. Why not?'

The worry drained from Eduardo's face as he saw her enthusiasm increase. Then horrible reality doused Katie's dreams.

'Oh—I've just realised I'll have to say no after all, Eduardo.' She made a little moue of understanding as the PA's face fell again. 'It's a horrible excuse, but I really *don't* have anything to wear. I came here to work, not party, so there's nothing suitable in my luggage. We must be miles from the nearest dress shop, so it isn't as though I could nip out and buy something, even if I *liked* clothes shopping.'

Eduardo sympathised with her disappointment, but then stopped. Suddenly, he began looking Katie up and down as though calculating her size. Then he beamed. His smile became so wide his eyes almost disappeared behind his plump pink cheeks.

'Ah! I may be able to do something about that, Miss Carter. Come with me—but not a word to the Count.'

They walked along the second floor balcony. Dark, gloomy portraits glowered from every wall. Katie noticed some discreetly placed buckets beneath a glazed dome, high above. Something other than sunshine must stream down from those leaded lights when it rained. Eduardo pointed out Giovanni's private suite as they passed. Twenty metres further along the corridor, they stopped at an identical mahogany door and Eduardo unlocked it. With one touch to its highly polished brass handle, the door swung open.

Katie was ushered into a shadowy suite. The fragrance of beeswax polish that wafted through the rest of the villa had no escape from these shuttered, half forgotten rooms. It mingled with the memory of expensive perfumes and new things. Eduardo went over to the windows. Folding back the shutters, he let sunlight pour in. The suite was set out like Katie's own, but on a much grander scale, and its furniture was covered with dust-sheets. She got some idea of its character from glimpses of upholstery peeping out from beneath the covers. It was all very pink and gold—and fluffy. Her mind never far from her work, Katie decided this place would go down in her notes as the 'Pink Princess Suite'.

'Now, if you would care to follow me, Miss Carter.' Eduardo crossed the drawing room and went through a door into the bedroom beyond. Like the old 'entertainment suite,' this was almost completely white. Instead of being circular, the bed here was an empress-sized rectangle. Its dust-cover had slipped and Katie caught sight of a white silk headboard, deeply buttoned with large gold nuggets. She was almost lost for words. Her mind went straight back to the alteration that had been made to the Amato family tree. She had a dozen questions, but Eduardo's expression warned her not to pry.

'This is nice…' was the only comment she could think to make.

Eduardo said nothing. Katie waited for him to give her some clues about the room's most recent occupant. He did not. Instead, he moved into a dressing room half the size of Katie's own suite. Fitted cupboards took up one whole wall. They were painted in a high gloss white, with details picked out in gold. Uncovering a dressing table, he took a keypad from its drawer. Opening the white suede case, he revealed ranks of small gold keys, each marked with a white identifying tag.

'Now, Miss Carter, let us consider. It is early summer, so that means we should be looking in Range Two…' His finger hovered across the second leaf of the keypad. 'Hmm, for dinner on the yacht—a nautical theme, perhaps, so that means the blues and greens…' Running down the rows of tiny labels, he selected a key. Approaching one of the cupboard doors, he opened it.

Katie's eyes widened. Inside the closet hung more clothes than she had owned in her whole life. Each was stored in a clear protective cover. It was all filed in strict colour code, from palest sky-blue to midnight velvet.

'Which would you prefer—trousers and a top? That seems to be your style. You can mix and match from dozens of those.'

Katie could believe it.

'Or there are skirts—'

'I think it had better be a dress, Eduardo. I don't usually wear them, but this sounds like a formal affair.'

'When the Count throws a party, it always is.'

'Then it should be full-length,' Katie decided.

Eduardo looked more pleased by the minute. His smile gave Katie the courage to ask a question.

'Eduardo, why doesn't everyone refer to Signor Amato as 'The Count' when he is not at work?'

'Because he stopped using his official title altogether when—'

He brought himself up short, and began again.

'—The Count stopped using his title when it became obvious he would be the last of his line.'

That partly explained the alteration to the panel in the Smoking Gallery. It also set alarm bells ringing inside Katie's head.

'Wait a minute, Eduardo. Whose clothes *are* these?'

'They belonged to the late Contessa, Miss Carter. Signor Giovanni decreed that she should be erased from his life. That is why only his name appears on the Amato family tree now. It seemed too hasty a decision at the time, to me. His father was still alive then and living here as count…so I persuaded him to have everything transported here from Signor Giovanni's marital home in Milan. I did it in case he ever regretted destroying the Contessa's things completely. Up until now he has not, but you never know…' he added quickly, putting a finger to his lips. Katie did not need the warning. Eduardo's voice was firm enough to block any more questions heading in that direction, but her nerves sent her down another route.

'I can't possibly wear a dead woman's clothes!' she announced.

'Why not? The Contessa Lia has no more use for them.'
The reply shocked her.

'What in the world will Signor Amato say if I appear dressed as his wife? I suppose the Contessa Lia *was* his wife?'

Eduardo gave her an uncomfortable smile.

'She must have looked really lovely in all these beautiful designer things. Oh, that poor man.' Katie shook her head in dismay, but Eduardo laughed.

'The Count scorns sympathy, Miss Carter. And he would not recognise anything from this collection. Everything here is brand-new. Look—the ones that are not handmade still have their price tags in place. The Contessa rarely wore anything more than once, if at all. Ensembles were either sent back to their designer after use or thrown away. Very occasionally she would take a particular fancy to something. Then it would be cleaned and filed...' He pointed towards a smaller but still impressive range of closets on another wall.

Katie went on staring as Eduardo flicked through the clothes with the air of an expert. He pulled out a lilac sheath, held it up against her, frowned and put it back. This was repeated with several more beautiful dresses. Katie had never thought she would be reluctant to get her hands on the work of Ferragamo and the rest but her mind was filled with doubts. Any woman who could wear clothes like these must have been absolutely drop-dead gorgeous. How on earth could she possibly compete tonight? *Not that Count Giovanni Amato could ever be expected to look twice at a commoner like me,* she thought, and then stopped. Eduardo had reached a dress that made them both sigh. It was cut from sapphire silk taffeta, discreetly spangled with bugle beads. He lifted it out with reverence. They both nodded. Katie knew this was The One. He handed it to her and she gazed in admiration, then turned for the door, believing the search was over.

'Wait! You cannot try it on yet, Miss Carter—we haven't been through the green section. And what about your shoes and accessories?'

By the time Eduardo had run through the 'palest mint to laurel' cupboard, she was agonising as much as he was over the final choice.

'In the green strapless lamé you would look like a mermaid, Miss Carter. Especially if you wore your hair loose around your shoulders.' Eduardo admired the gloss on the auburn braid she wore while working.

'But I always keep my hair tied back. And on the other hand—the blue silk makes rather less of a statement…' Katie mused. She was still not at all sure which dress to go for. 'Remember, Eduardo, I am not a proper guest. I should be discreet. I am only attending to make up the numbers.'

He gave her another strange look. 'Yes…' he allowed, 'and as such jewellery will present a problem at the moment. It would not be right to ask Signor Amato if you could use something from the historic Amato collection. Hmm…' He tapped his teeth with the keypad. Then he had a brainwave. 'I know, while you prepare for the party, I shall ask around among the female staff. The Count pays good wages. I'm sure someone will be more than happy to lend you a few trinkets for such a good cause.'

'You mentioned that this was a charity event,' Katie said as Eduardo looked her out a pair of cream leather stilettos and a matching purse. 'Which one is the Count supporting tonight?'

'His own foundation, set up to study the causes of still-birth.' Quick as a flash, Eduardo threw a cashmere shawl across the gowns lying in Katie's arms. 'There. That will set off either ensemble most elegantly.'

It was a masterstroke. Katie was dazzled. She was halfway back to her suite before she realised that Eduardo must have filled her arms with luxury to stop her asking any more awkward questions.

CHAPTER FOUR

Two hours later, Giovanni strode down to the grand entrance hall of the Villa Antico. He was expecting a long wait, but as he checked his Rolex he heard a door closing on the upper floor. He had time to straighten his cuff-links and adjust his tie in the cheval-glass beside the front doors before anybody came into view behind his reflection. Then he stopped and turned. A complete stranger was walking along the landing and it was the most glamorous vision he had ever seen. Then with a jolt he realised it was Miss Katie Carter. For long moments he relished her approach, holding his breath. Then she reached the top of the stairs and realised he was watching her.

Seeing the look on his face was enough to make her hesitate at the top. He was gazing at her with rapt, unswerving attention and it was wonderful.

Giovanni took his time, appreciating her slender beauty. Framed against the faded splendour of his house, it was the ideal contrast between austerity and soft, pliant loveliness. That blue silk dress showed off her creamy skin and delicate collar-bones to perfection. At her slightest movement, a provocative slit in its side seam revealed that her legs really *did* go sky-high. He cleared his throat and stepped forward.

Unprofessional arousal was haunting him again. The antidote was to break his own awestruck silence.

'Miss Carter—over the past centuries queens, contessas and courtesans have used that staircase. You inherit their tradition beautifully.'

'Thank you, Signor Amato.' Katie took it as a compliment, revelling in his smile. She had been nervous, but now his words gave her a rush of confidence. Suddenly she felt more like a princess than an interior designer. Surely anything was possible on a night like this. Taking a deep breath, she raised her head, put her shoulders back and tried to descend like a true consort. He watched her every heartbeat and it gave her more courage. In return, she could not take her eyes off him. He was perfectly groomed as always, but instead of the shirt-sleeves in which he usually worked, he was dressed in a three-piece suit. Seeing him in such a formal outfit made Katie realise what a serious event this was going to be. Nerves threatened to overwhelm her again and she wondered if her palms were damp.

'Stop there for a moment,' he said as she reached the ground floor. For a few agonising seconds he was silent, studying her from every angle. His face never lost its expression of wonder and eventually he nodded. 'Yes…'

Everything was contained in the way he said that single word. Katie almost collapsed with relief.

'Oh, thank goodness! When I couldn't decide between this dress and the green one—'

That broke the spell. He put his hands on his hips and whistled. 'Miss Carter, you amaze me. I never imagined a sensible, working woman like you would pack more than one formal gown for a stay here.' His expression of amazement quickly became a wry smile. 'Nevertheless you certainly look the part tonight, Miss Carter.' He paused. 'I must warn you, however, that parties are not my first love. I *never* entertain formally at my properties, and only rarely on my yacht.' She caught his gaze and saw a twinkling in his eye. 'But when I do, Miss Carter, it is usually quite an evening.'

Katie felt a sudden return of spirit. Tonight she would be part of his world.

One of the Amato limousines was waiting for them outside. Katie automatically went towards the rear passenger door, but Giovanni placed a hand on her arm to stop her. She jumped at his touch and looked up at him in alarm. Their eyes met, but before either could speak the chauffeur had opened the car door and was waiting for her to step in. Katie moved forward again. Giovanni's fingers fell from her wrist, but their touch lingered like fire. It almost made her forget the promise she had made to the indoor staff.

'Oh—wait—I must just…' One foot inside the carpeted luxury of the car, she stopped and looked around at the façade of the grand old house. Dark shapes were moving behind the muslin curtains at several windows. Raising a hand, Katie waved. The crystal earrings and blue beaded choker she had been loaned were not the genuine article, but they glittered and sparkled in the evening sunlight like the real thing.

'I'm actually beginning to enjoy this,' Giovanni said, watching her settle herself inside his car. 'Now *there's* something I never thought would happen.'

The chauffeur shut the car door between them before Katie could reply. She had to wait until Giovanni got in beside her before answering.

'Why do you hold parties if you don't like them, Signor?' she enquired as they were wafted away from the villa.

Giovanni looked out of his window. If she saw him smile now, she might think he was smug, condescending, or both. That was not his intention.

'They are the price one should pay for living like this.' He indicated the limousine's interior. It was plush with upholstery and fragrant from a tiny flower arrangement set on the rear parcel shelf. 'I use my money to try and make others part with theirs. Sometimes it is business. Tonight it is in the interests of charity, which makes it doubly important. The more we can persuade them to pledge this evening, Miss Carter, the happier I shall be.' When he looked at her now, his face was touched with genuine warmth. Despite her nerves, Katie found it easy to respond.

'Then I shall need some information on your guest, Signor Balzone, if I am to play my part properly.'

'He is a media man, Miss Carter, and extremely wealthy. His goodwill means a great deal, so we need to charm him like he has never been charmed before.'

'I am surprised you are bothered by the fact he is rich,' Katie said as their car drove sedately towards the helipad. 'I would have thought a successful man like you could have funded any number of good causes single-handed, Signor Amato.'

'Financial success is not everything in life, Miss Carter.'

He might have donated a smile at this point, she thought. He did not.

'If Agosto Balzone enjoys himself this evening, he could become an important sponsor of my charity.' Giovanni stretched out his long legs and brushed an invisible speck from his suit. 'He may also give us free publicity and airtime, cheaper advertising rates, or all three.'

'So Signor Balzone has only been invited to this party because he can do you some good?' Katie enquired slowly. It sounded a horrible ploy.

'That is the only reason anyone is ever invited anywhere, Miss Carter. To be brutal, it is why you are sitting next to me now rather than stuck in your suite, poring over your plans for my house.'

In that moment her romantic dreams faltered and died. Her Cinderella fantasy must end here. Tonight was going to be 'business as usual' when it came to their relationship.

Fine—that's just the way I like it, Katie thought. Or at least, it was…

'It is an approach, I suppose,' she said warily. 'Well, I shall do my best to help your plans, Signor Amato.'

'Good.' There was real appreciation in his voice as he opened a flap in the limousine's interior. It revealed a glittering, fully stocked mini-bar. 'I appreciate it is asking a lot of you, Miss Carter, to hold your own in an assembly full of strangers. But please remember, I am extremely grateful for the way you have stepped in at the last moment. If you feel unhappy or uncertain about anything at all, you can always look to me for help.'

'Don't worry, I'm determined to enjoy myself,' Katie responded. 'Although I want to do more than just make up the numbers at your party.'

Giovanni looked at her acutely as he offered her a drink. 'You will be careful though, won't you, Miss Carter? What you get up to overnight is your own affair, of course, but as your host I feel responsible for you. If there is the slightest hint of a problem you must come straight to me. I don't want you to feel pressurised by anyone, in any way. Not even by me,' he added mischievously.

Katie accepted a glass of fresh orange juice, but with caution in her eyes. 'You've worried me now. Eduardo said this was a dinner,' she said with slow meaning. 'He never mentioned anything about "overnight".'

Giovanni looked perplexed. 'It would not have occurred to him that there was anything worth explaining. I can hardly expect guests to come from far and wide without offering them the chance of an overnight stay.' He made it sound like the most natural thing in the world.

Katie was troubled. '*I* won't be expected to stay though, will I?'

'Of course,' he said nonchalantly.

He clearly did not expect Katie to need things spelled out. In the face of his certainty she began to feel nervous again. 'I knew that you sometimes spent time on your yacht but I never expected to be included.'

'Didn't you?' At that point the corners of his mouth almost lifted, but his eyes remained wary. Katie remembered the office gossip about his love-life and realised that a lot of women probably tried to play the innocent with him.

'No, I didn't,' she said firmly. 'If I had, I would have made sure I brought more than this purse. Some perfume, lipstick and a handkerchief are hardly going to see me through a stay on a luxury yacht, are they?'

'An overnight case has been packed for you. It is stowed away in the back.' He tipped his head towards the rear of the car.

Katie was aghast. 'How on earth did you know what I might need?'

'I didn't.' Giovanni took a sip of chilled mineral water. 'That is Eduardo's job.'

Katie was not convinced. 'I'm not sure I like the idea of relying on someone else to pack my bag for me.'

'I think you may be pleasantly surprised, Miss Carter. Eduardo has never let me down yet.'

'Yes, but you're a man.'

'So you've noticed?' Giovanni leaned forward to check that

the intercom connecting them to the driver was switched off, a smile haunting his lips. 'My father always suspected that Eduardo was not interested in women. You should have no worries there.'

Katie thought of Eduardo's expertise in kitting her out for the evening. 'So—is Eduardo gay?'

'I neither know nor care.' Giovanni looked at her as though she had suggested he should move to Siena. 'Eduardo has been an excellent employee for many years. Before I inherited, he saved the house of Amato from many scandals. Discretion is everything, Miss Carter.' He took another drink and looked out of the window.

They were not in the car for long, driving only as far as the estate's airstrip where a pilot had the Amato helicopter ready for take-off. Their seats were deep, roomy and comfortable but Katie did not have much time to get used to her luxurious surroundings. The horizon soon became a glittering line. As they flew towards the coast, the usual perfume of hot herbs took on a seaside tang.

'Oh, look! The beach!' Katie said in excitement, before she could stop herself.

'Enjoy the view, I'm afraid we won't be able to stop and visit, Miss Carter.' Giovanni laughed. 'Some of my guests might want to venture ashore, but I doubt it. They visit me for a break from that kind of life. Viareggio is too busy for my liking. In the past, I have seen far too much damage done by the relentless pursuit of pleasure. I prefer to keep it at a distance, myself.'

Katie wondered what he meant. Her childhood had been spent listening to her mother hankering after things she could not have. Perhaps there had been some of that going on in his life, too.

'I just assumed your boat would be parked in a marina.' She looked puzzled.

'My *Viola* is hardly a boat, Miss Carter,' he said with quiet pride. 'She is moored offshore. That gives good views of the coastline, but it is a long way from the holidaymakers and paparazzi lenses.'

'I can understand why you like that,' she said with a sigh, 'but it would have been nice to feel the sand between my toes for once. I haven't been on a beach for ages.'

'Then you shall visit the seashore beside *Viola*'s pool, Miss Carter.'

She laughed, imagining a heap of grit beside a hot tub— and then she saw where the helicopter was going to land. It was spiralling down towards a vast ship. Katie stared out of the window as they landed on a dedicated flight deck that was large enough to house at least two other helicopters.

'This isn't a yacht—it's—it's an ocean liner!'

'Oh, hardly that, Miss Carter,' Giovanni said affably as a member of his crew helped them out on to the deck. 'Show Miss Carter to her allotted suite, Guido. How is life with little Pepito now? Are you and Maria managing to get any sleep yet?'

'Not a lot, Signor, but at least Maria has my company here, overnight.' The young man gave a rueful laugh. 'Thank you for letting her come with me this week—it would have been hard for her, looking after a new baby at home, alone.'

'Don't mention it, Guido. A father's first duty should always be towards his wife and child. Now, I haven't checked my emails since this morning so I am off to the office. As for Miss Carter, she has a desire to see the pool. Give her directions to it, would you?'

With that he was gone, absorbed by work again. Katie tried out an uncertain smile on Guido. 'I'm just an interior designer. I'm not with Signor Amato…in any meaningful sense,' she ventured.

'Of course not, Miss Carter.' Guido smiled.

As he led her to her room, Katie used the opportunity to try and find out a little more about Giovanni and his past. But, as she questioned Guido, she realised Amato staff members were beyond such tricks. Even though she found out nothing, the loyalty Giovanni obviously inspired in his staff impressed her.

Guido led her along yet another corridor, his footsteps muffled by thick carpet and efficient air conditioning. 'Here is your suite, Miss Carter. The pool is down the corridor to the left.' He unlocked the door and stood back, holding out the key. Katie took it, realising she was not going to find out any more. Thanking him, she went inside to explore her new surroundings.

Her suite was only slightly smaller than the one at the villa. Instead of plasterwork, the interior here was oak panelling, polished to a glassy shine. Soft upholstery and heavy velvet curtains made it feel like a luxury hotel rather than a ship. Katie's rooms looked out towards the shore, which was bright with all the colour and noise of early summer. She had wondered why Giovanni never looked genuinely happy, but perhaps now she had a hint of his reality. Although he had all the wealth, status and 'boy's toys' that any man could ever want, his past had injured him in some way. Katie realised now that money really could not buy happiness.

She checked over her luggage quickly, marvelling that Eduardo had put in everything she could possibly need, and more. Then she set off for a look round. Before Guido had left her, he had asked if she would like drinks served by the pool. Katie had been delighted by the idea. She was even more excited when she reached it. The *Viola* really was equipped with a beach of silvery sand as well as a deep blue pool, and waiting beneath the shade of an awning was Giovanni. As she approached he offered her a glass of chilled champagne. The sand rushed into her borrowed stilettos as she crossed the beach towards him, but she hardly noticed.

'Do we really have time for this, Signor?'

'There is *always* time for Taittinger '95. Force yourself, Miss Carter,' he teased. 'It is well worth the effort.'

She raised her glass to take a sip, but he stopped her. 'Wait. We should have a toast in anticipation of your triumph this evening. I have every confidence that this party will be an astounding success.' He touched his glass against hers. The pure crystal rang with quality and Katie took a first taste. He joined her and they both savoured the champagne's lemon and almond fireworks. Then he raised his glass again. 'And now to you, Miss Carter: for not only making up the numbers, but for doing so in such spectacular fashion.'

They drank, and he topped up her glass with another foaming meringue of bubbles.

Katie wondered why no other man had ever affected her as Giovanni Amato did. Her sympathy for his shadowy past was only a tiny part of it. One look from him, and it was all forgotten. His gaze made her feel as though she—a working-class nobody—was the only person in the universe. Common sense tried to tell her that he must look at all women in this way. That was the way good manners and charm worked—but sense didn't have much to do with the way Katie was feeling. Then the trill of Giovanni's phone alerted him.

'They're here,' he began, but before Katie's nerves could get the better of her he shot her a conspiratorial smile. 'You'll find that anticipation is the worst part. It'll be OK once we're up and running. Just remember—they've come here for a good time, not a long time. Sometimes that's the only thought that keeps me going. That, and the sparkling medicine out of these bottles, of course. Have another dose.' As Katie giggled, he filled her glass again.

As they left the spa area to stroll along to the observation deck, Katie realised something strange. It was the first time she had been alone with a man without feeling the urge to fill every pause in his conversation with nervous chatter. Today she was happy to stay silent and absorb the drift of Giovanni's clean, cool fragrance on the breeze.

The air and sea around the *Viola* became busy. So many helicopters and launches arriving within minutes of each other would have thrown anywhere else into chaos. It did not happen on Giovanni Amato's yacht. Everything was managed smoothly and without fuss. Katie was alight with nerves, but once all the guests had embarked there was no time to be shy. She swung into full personality mode. It was something that the naturally shy Katie had trained herself to do. To succeed in her line of business, she had to make herself sell ideas to rich people. The only difference between her work and this party was Giovanni Amato.

For Giovanni's part, he was encouraged by the way she tried to adapt to her unusual role. Although busy with his guests, he took every chance to glance over at her. At first he was relieved to see her laughing, or nodding in response to an anecdote. Then a faint unease began to creep over him. The audience gathered around her was mostly male. What had he done? She didn't deserve to be cornered. This was, after all, only Miss Katie Carter. She was a working woman, unused to the high life and the way it was lived. He frowned. She was his contractor, and an unusually retiring one at that. Tonight she was also his guest. Unlike the others, she was doing him a personal favour by being here, not a financial one. It all made him feel strangely protective towards her.

As long as she did not look at her host, Katie could sparkle like the sea. She concentrated on being pleasant but discreet. Then Signor Balzone was announced at the door. Giovanni was at her side in an instant.

'You're doing a great job,' he whispered as their guest of honour approached.

'Are you sure?'

'Believe me, the Princess Miadora herself couldn't do any better.'

This time, Katie did not have to make any effort to smile as Giovanni introduced her. His protective hand, nestling in the small of her back as he drew her forward, saw to that. Her warm glow increased as Agosto Balzone began talking to them. He had seen the work she had done for several other clients, and was delighted to meet her. Katie could hardly believe her luck. Keeping this man happy would be easy. He already liked her work and his interest was genuine.

Giovanni did not share her relief. As Katie began to relax, he found himself becoming strangely tense. Conversations about commodities and hedge funds held little interest for him now. His mind kept drifting over to where Katie was being monopolised by a fat, balding man who had more ex-wives than sense.

She was so beautiful, and Balzone was such a rogue.

Giovanni wondered if he ought to warn her of the man's reputation. It was only to stop her getting hurt, he told himself, and that made sense. He was beginning to realise that a girl like Katie could have her pick of any man in the room, despite her humble beginnings. He knew he should have felt pleased at giving her such an opportunity. Instead it irritated him. He put it down to his own dislike of being paired off.

The whole company progressed to the ballroom, where drinks and canapés were served. Katie was enjoying herself hugely, especially when Giovanni materialised at her side. Cupping her elbow with one hand, he drew her aside gently.

'I am concerned for you, Miss Carter. Balzone is to be charmed, but not at the expense of everyone else.' He pursed his lips. 'Take care you do not get out of your depth.'

'I can manage, thank you,' Katie said firmly, plunging back into the assembly. She had not expected to be patronised for doing as she was told. Giovanni's words burned, and her only remedy was to charm everyone. It was difficult to memorise all the names, but luckily a few of the faces were familiar from her work. One was a client, and several others had visited the Villa Adriatica while she had been working there. Katie managed to circulate, smile and delight them all. When a uniformed maid announced that dinner was about to be served, Agosto Balzone took her arm and escorted her into the dining room like a princess.

Katie expected to shuffle around, looking for her name on a place card. Instead, she was ushered straight to a seat at one end of an enormous dining table. Giovanni, she noticed, was positioned at exactly the opposite end. Signor Balzone was seated on Katie's right, while the young man on her left was introduced as one of Giovanni's distant cousins from Milan.

The seating plan had split couples up and scattered them around the table, to help conversation. Katie found Agosto Balzone great fun, but Cousin Severino Amato was a different matter. He was an archaeologist, and as nervous as only a scientist on a yacht full of money could be. As another outsider, Katie got on with him really well. Then she realised that Giovanni's eyes were haunting her all the way from his position at the head of the table.

* * *

Time sauntered by with no one taking any notice of the clock. Only when Signor Balzone showed signs of flagging did Giovanni call for more coffee. The guests who were not staying overnight used this as an excuse to leave. Katie slipped away to her suite as soon as it was polite to do so, but she could not stay there for long. Something about the salty breeze blowing through the open windows made her feel reckless. Instead of getting ready for bed, she decided to go for a walk around the deck. Coming out through the spa area, she found it lit by starlight. It was so idyllic she had a sudden urge to go and lie on a sun-lounger and look up into the velvety night sky. Stepping out on to the pool surround, she closed the door behind her with a loud click before realising she was not alone.

Giovanni Amato was leaning over the ship's rail. Glass in hand, he was gazing across the bay to where lights twinkled along the coast like a string of beads.

He turned at the sound of the door closing and saw her. There could be no escape.

'Good evening again, Miss Carter. So your admirers have finally let you go?'

Katie had been conscious of his watchful gaze all evening. It had been a support when her nerves flagged, but she did not like this hint that she might have been doing her job *too* well.

'Agosto is really nice. I'm going to the Uffizi Gallery with him next week. He knows how to get in without having to queue for hours.'

He raised an eyebrow mockingly. 'I could have told you that.'

'Oh. Then I'm sorry you didn't, Signor Amato.'

He took a sip of cognac and smiled. 'I'm amazed you can manage sightseeing, with your busy schedule.'

'I think it will be fun. Everyone is entitled to some time off,' Katie continued, unaware that she was being teased. She wondered whether to tell him it would not be a date with Balzone, but rather a foursome with good intentions. Like her, Agosto Balzone had felt sorry for their fellow dinner guest, Severino, the fish-out-of-water. Agosto was going to ask his bookish young niece along on the gallery trip, supposedly to make up the numbers.

Katie was beginning to think Giovanni Amato was the only member of the monied classes who wasn't obsessed by matchmaking.

'I suppose Balzone has offered to make you the star of his television company.'

She tilted her chin in defiance. 'No, he hasn't. And even if he had, Signor Amato, I wouldn't be interested.'

'I must admit to being relieved, Miss Carter. As I told you before: you are a guest in our country living under my roof, and you are an attractive young woman. I have to protect you.'

Katie seethed. Wine with dinner and the many compliments she had received from his guests had buoyed her up enough to challenge him. 'Don't you think that's a rather old-fashioned view, Signor Amato?'

'Good sense never goes out of fashion, Miss Carter.'

'You can call me Katie, you know. All your grand guests were quite happy to call me by my Christian name this evening, and vice versa,' she recalled with a touch of pride at having managed to blur the class divide.

'That is true,' he allowed. He took another sip of his drink and then looked at the remaining contents of the glass. There was so little left he downed the last drops in one go, then stood upright. 'Indeed, everyone remarked to me that you were the perfect hostess, Katie. Even finding time for that poor lad Severino.'

'There was a reason for that.' Katie shivered in the cool

night air. 'I've heard that you're full of scorn for people who try to set you up with single girls. Poor Severino couldn't imagine why he was attending your dinner, but I knew only too well. His fortune-seeking mother dragged him here. She brought her son in the hope of finding him a well-connected single girl—you could see it in her eyes.'

'Now before you go any further, Miss Carter, I should tell you that the "fortune-seeking mother" and I share a much loved great-uncle,' Giovanni interrupted her with a chuckle. 'May I take it, then, that you frown upon gold-diggers and all their works too?' Pushing himself away from the rail, he placed his empty glass on the nearest table.

Katie thought of her mother. Biology was the only thing she had in common with that woman, who had run away in pursuit of a bigger bank balance when things got tough. 'I certainly do, Signor Amato. I am afraid I have seen far too much chasing after money to have any respect for the people who do it.' She sighed.

'You don't know what a relief it is to find someone who thinks like that.' He smiled and, before Katie knew what was happening, his hands were on her shoulders, gently drawing her close.

'Thank you so much for making this evening a success, Katie. And for being so beautiful,' he breathed, brushing the lightest of kisses against her cheek.

Her heart stood still. This couldn't be happening—and yet it was. His fingers were still resting lightly on her silk-clad shoulders. She could not move. The slightest disturbance might cause him to release her and, with a pang, she realised she wanted to stay like this for ever.

They stood on deck, alone. Giovanni had intended the kiss as nothing more than a gesture of thanks, but something was happening deep within him. Tonight Miss Katie Carter had been transformed into a desirable young woman. He was seeing her with new eyes and it was drawing him across an invisible boundary. Now he was actually touching this different reality. It was novelty, delight and wonder all wrapped up in the warm mystery of a Mediterranean night

Until that moment, Giovanni had spent his entire life being sensible. Suddenly, sense was no longer enough. He needed this woman and drew her into his arms. At the exact moment her mouth opened in surprise, he covered it with his own.

Katie almost lost consciousness with the surging power of dreams come true. She had fantasised so often about sliding her hands over those powerful shoulders and being crushed against him like a possession. Now it was happening. For moments on end she revelled in the delicious feeling of having her own desire returned with interest. He was moulding her willing form to his body, caressing away her inhibitions. Any moment now, Katie knew he would break down the last of her reserve and possess her, bringing her to a state where she would give her all, willingly...

And then a terrible thought arrowed through her misty mind.

This was just the typical end to a typical dinner party for the world's most desirable man.

How many other girls had been here and done this?

Within seconds, Katie's dream tumbled into a nightmare. She had to stop him. Her principles as well as her morals were at stake. If she let him carry on like this, she would never be able to look him—or any other male client—in the eyes again. To jeopardise everything she had worked for in a moment of weakness would be fatal.

With almost superhuman strength, she forced herself from his arms.

The moment Giovanni felt her resistance he released her,

shocked. She had melted into him. She responded to his kiss in a way that had wiped all other thoughts and memories from his mind. And now she was pushing him away.

She stood before him now like a Cinderella of the high seas, wide-eyed, beautiful and as astonished as he was about what had happened.

Her initial reaction to his kiss had been adult and wanton. Now she looked like a little girl. This was not how it should be. He had spent the whole evening concerned about her vulnerability, but in the end *he* had been the bad guy. He had betrayed her trust.

Now it was up to him to rescue the situation. He brushed the back of his hand softly down her cheek, the tender action making her shiver. 'Good night, Katie Carter,' he said softly and then turned his back on fourteen generations of wanton Amato forebears and walked off to his stateroom.

CHAPTER FIVE

KATIE felt the magical touch of his lips all night. Her dreams fired by fantasies, she woke early, with a feverish ache that needed to be cooled. The ideal cure would be to spend some time in the on-board swimming pool, but she was nervous. Despite the fact that the *Viola* was a large ship, it was a small space in which to avoid anyone. Particularly when the person in question put in a hundred lengths or so each morning.

She spent ages weighing up the likelihood of Giovanni choosing exactly the same moment she did to take a swim. Then she thought of the more alarming prospect of Agosto Balzone seeing her in a bikini and decided against going to the pool at all. Their guest of honour had done nothing over dinner to suggest he was anything but a perfect gentleman, but Giovanni had warned her about him. On balance, Katie decided it was safer to keep out of everyone's way. She took breakfast in her room, but could hardly manage a mouthful. Her mind was full of Giovanni and he left no room for anything else.

Life on board the yacht was beyond anything she had experienced before. One maid collected her laundry, while a second laid out her clothes for the day and ran her a deep bubbly bath. Katie lay in the water and tried out a thousand different ways of acting towards Giovanni when they sat next to each other for the flight home. She tried to tell herself she had done the right thing. A man like Giovanni could have any girl he wanted and probably did. He had respected her when she'd called a halt. All she needed to do was put it down to experience, as he would. When she next met him, she ought to act as though nothing had happened. It had been a mutual mistake, nothing more.

The trouble was, Katie could not convince herself of that. She now knew she would sacrifice everything for this man. There had been nothing wrong about his kiss—it had been perfect. Her only regret was that she had ended it.

While she fretted, everything that would not be required until her arrival back at the Villa Antico was packed away. By the time Katie emerged from the bathroom, her suite had been completely valeted. Fresh flower arrangements were in place and her suitcase stood beside the door. The whole operation had been carried out with the minimum fuss and the maximum efficiency.

Katie sat on a velvet chaise longue and flicked through the selection of glossy magazines supplied for her. It was hopeless. If there had been full colour photographs of Bigfoot riding an UFO she would not have noticed. The only pictures going through her mind involved Giovanni. Kissing him had been an unbelievable experience. Desperately, she tried to convince herself it had been a dream. That did not work. Then she told herself imagination had blown the whole event out of proportion. She did everything to rationalise her thoughts before her next meeting with Giovanni, but there was no cure.

Katie had tasted paradise and she was greedy for more.

The time came for her to set off for the flight deck. She checked her appearance in the mirror a dozen times. There was nothing left of the glamorous creature who had felt Giovanni's kiss the night before. Her hair was pulled back from her face and trapped in its usual plait. She was wearing her normal practical-but-dull working clothes of black trousers, matching jacket and plain white top. Her borrowed jewellery was carefully hidden away. Katie tried to pace herself on the long walk from her suite to the helicopter. In reality she was fizzing with anticipation. Would she be lucky enough to be greeted with another kiss? She blushed, knowing that this time she would not be able to resist. It was all she had been thinking of, night and morning. His lips on hers, and the warmth of his touch matching the heat of her newly discovered passion…

When she reached the helipad, Giovanni was already deep in conversation with the pilot. She looked around, hoping that conditions would mean they could not fly. Another day spent with Giovanni on the *Viola*, beside his pool…

She was to be disappointed in more ways than one. The weather was perfect for flying, and Giovanni acknowledged her with nothing more than a casual nod.

'Good morning, Katie.'

Her ready smile faded with this everyday greeting.

'*I* shall be flying us back to the Villa Antico. There seems little point in using Ugo again, when he has work to do here on board ship,' he announced, carefully helping Katie up into the body of the aircraft before she had time to say anything.

'…I am sorry about last night, Katie,' he murmured as soon as they were alone. Taking his place in the pilot's seat, he immersed himself in pre-flight checks. 'It was very wrong of me to take advantage of your good nature. It should never have happened.'

After that, they travelled in a communications blackout. He

was concentrating on getting them back to the Villa Antico. Katie could not trust herself to speak, so she used the time for reflection. Giovanni had sounded as though he regretted what he had done, and she was suffering for it. Screwing her handkerchief into a ball, she tried to transfer all her pain and rage into it. She had been right all along. People were trouble. The minute you let them affect you, it was the end.

She squeezed so hard that her nails bit right through the fabric and into the palms of her hands. In front of her, Giovanni adopted perfect pilot practice. He kept a lookout in all directions—except hers. He spoke to his radio—but not to Katie. His hands moved about the control panel with all the swift assurance she wanted him to use on her body.

It was too much. By the time the groves and avenues of the Villa Antico swung into view, Katie had worked herself up into indignant fury. How dared this man toy with her emotions and then act as though nothing had happened? She would show him!

No woman had ever turned Giovanni down before. It was uncharted territory for him. He had spent a sleepless night wondering what was wrong with her. Their silent journey home made him realise that the only way to find out for sure was to ask her directly.

He did not get the chance. As soon as they touched down, Katie jumped out of the helicopter and marched off towards the villa without a backward glance. He stood and watched her go.

All the doors in the villa were standing wide open. Katie felt a refreshing breeze cool her hot cheeks as she went towards Eduardo's office. A door banged somewhere, a distant telephone rang. She did not notice. All she wanted to do was hand in her borrowed jewellery and get back to her one true friend—work.

'Here she is—the belle of the ball.' Eduardo was sitting behind his desk, as smug as a cat.

'I was hardly that.' Katie made a face as she handed over the earrings and necklace for him to return.

'On the contrary, Miss Carter, incoming emails and calls have told me all I need to know about your triumph. You charmed them all. As well as playing your part, I have a feeling you have given Carter Interiors some good publicity.'

'It was *supposed* to be a fund-raising evening, Eduardo.'

'Don't worry—it was a success on every level. You were a star, and the Amato Foundation has received promises running into hundreds of thousands of euros. The only person who did not mention you at all was Mrs Dale-Carr. She said she was ringing up to thank Signor Amato for last night's little soirée, but *I* know she was calling on the off chance of speaking to him directly. That woman is intent on luring him over to her home in the USA for a holiday.'

'I guessed as much. It was impossible not to hear her telling Signor Amato how much he would enjoy the chance of a break on her ranch.'

'That goes to show how little she understands him.' Eduardo thrust out his lower lip in disapproval. 'Signor Amato does not know the meaning of the word "holiday."'

Katie frowned. 'Mrs Dale-Carr is a widow who runs a large stud farm. In which case, Signor Amato should fit in there perfectly.'

It was a mistake. Eduardo's ears pricked up at the reference.

'Oh, yes?' There was suspicion in his voice. His head was on one side and he quizzed her silently.

'I've heard that seduction has been a popular hobby with some of the Amato clan, that's all,' Katie improvised, trying to stop any rumour before it could begin. The way she was feeling now would make whispers too painful to bear. Despite her smile, she was falling apart. Giovanni's moonlight kiss had proved to be nothing but a meaningless gesture and he had written it off as a mistake. He was a cold, hard, calculating machine.

So why did the thought of Giovanni with that Dale-Carr woman—with any woman—twist such a knife in her heart?

Because I've been falling in love with him since the first moment I saw him, Katie admitted to herself. *And when he finally reached out and touched me, it made things a million times worse. This awful feeling only comes from wanting something I cannot possibly have.*

That was the rational explanation. The trouble was, this irresistible man made her feel anything but rational.

For the next few weeks Katie did everything in her power to avoid the temptation called Giovanni Amato. She tried to stay away from him. Complete isolation from a client was impossible, but Katie did her best. Each time he interrupted her, she was quick to turn back to her work. She had to: the tremors that shot through her body each time she saw him were too powerful to be denied. Keeping her eyes averted from that taut, handsome body took all her concentration. And the thought of those wickedly delicious, but now grimly serious lips touched all her dreams.

It built into a record-breaking summer. Giovanni had all the doors and windows in the White Office thrown open each day to take advantage of any breeze. Business always took precedence with him, but on this particular day something was working away at the back of his mind like grit in an oyster. Tomorrow marked the end of Katie's stay. At the moment, she was making a last circuit of the villa. He could hear the reel of her tape as she checked measurements, her voice as she chatted with his staff or the sound of her footsteps on the gravel terrace outside.

Giovanni had almost reconciled himself to the slip he had made that night on the *Viola*. The way he saw it, he had acted in the heat of the moment. Now he was busy, and she was busy, too. Neither of them had any time at all for the other. That was how it should be, between employer and employee, he kept telling himself.

He stopped congratulating himself as he became aware that it had gone quiet. For some weeks his bleak, empty house had been filled with chatter and laughter. He had put this down to the staff bedding in with his regime. This return to silence was unsettling. Strangely disturbed, Giovanni found he could no longer concentrate on his work. Then suddenly, when he least expected it, there was a loud knock at the main door to his office. He glanced up. It was Katie.

'May I come in and do one last quick tour of your office, Signor Amato?'

Her cool detachment was utterly professional. Giovanni had to hand it to her. No one would have guessed that for a split second she had turned to liquid fire beneath his hands. The image of serious dedication she displayed now was complete except for one thing. She was staring at the threadbare Indian rugs as she made her request, not at him.

'Fine. Go right ahead.' He almost smiled as his words had the desired effect. She could not resist a quick glance at him. In that second, he saw the days fall away. Her lips parted and a blush coloured her usually pale skin. She was remembering. Knowing what was going through her mind pleased him strangely. He smiled at her. Heat rushed to her cheeks and, in her embarrassment, she did a clumsy, lightning circuit of his room. In her hurry to reach the furthest corner of his office, she managed to drop her box of tools. He bent to help her as she scrabbled to retrieve her things, but she had already hastily gathered them up. She thanked him quickly and left.

When she was gone, Giovanni stood up and went over to get himself a drink. As he poured the ice-cold water he noticed something white on the floor beneath his desk. It was a sheet of paper, which must have blown off his table in a draught between the open doors. He returned to his seat and picked it up. The top lolled heavily. He flipped it back and found that a weight of bills had been stapled to one corner. The word 'Unpaid' had been stamped across the top one. Concerned, Giovanni thumbed through the rest. They were all marked in the same way. Some were underlined in red, others added the words 'Final Demand.' Sitting down, he turned his attention to the letter accompanying these accusations. This must take top priority. Amato International had not received mail like this since his father's death, when Giovanni had been left to salvage the firm from approaching disaster.

The letter was scrawled in Biro. This was unusual for his business mail, but not unknown. Before reading it, he flicked through the receipts again. The first was from a garage. The rest were unpaid grocery, laundry and credit card slips. A horrible chill told him the letter must be intended for someone else. Turning back the tide of debt, he checked the final page. Instead of a signature, the single word 'Mummy' was underlined with a dozen kisses. Without reading anything else, he looked at the opening words of the letter. It was addressed to 'Dear Katie…'

He stood up. Katie's mother must be cast in the same mould as his own father. Life as an only son had taught Giovanni all he needed to know about spendthrifts. He had too much relevant experience to stand by and watch Katie suffer in the same way. His mind began to work. He had to say something to her, but what advice could he give? Every confrontation with his own father had piled on the pressure. Giovanni had heard every hard luck story, every promise and every threat. Fighting the same battles for years had hardened him until he'd developed a sob-proof shell. He thought of Katie's recent coldness towards him. Perhaps this explained it. Under constant threat from her mother's lifestyle, the same thing was already happening to her.

Giovanni knew he could not let it happen. Drumming the fingers of one hand on his desk, he stared down at the sheaf of demands. He had never managed to get his own father's wild living under control. What made him think he could advise Katie? Tomorrow was her final day here. Whatever he did, it would have to be quick. Without giving himself time to dwell on the rights and wrongs of his decision, Giovanni strode over and opened the door to his office. When he did, he was confronted by a vision.

Katie was looking out of one of the great windows that lined the upper hallway. Her hands were flat on the wide stone sill and she was frowning at something below in the grounds. A shaft of sunlight falling through the glass turned her hair into an amber halo. She turned and smiled at the sound of an approach, but the look vanished as she saw who it was.

'Signor Amato—what is it? What is wrong?'

For the first time in his life, Giovanni could not think what to say. He filled the void by holding up the letter, hoping she would rush forward and snatch the horrible thing from him. She did not. Instead she stayed where she was. The worry in her eyes was almost unbearable. Giovanni passed her the letter.

'I came out to give you this.' He paused, then chose to ease the tension by not dwelling on the letter's content right away. 'And to see what all the racket was about.'

She sighed gratefully. 'They've just finished putting up a marquee over by the helipad. Now there's some discussion about who's in charge of transporting all the tables and chairs over to it.'

'Ah, yes.' He joined her at the window. From here he could see Eduardo's small bald spot. He did not need to hear the conversation. Stefano was waving his arms about eloquently enough. 'That is for the staff party tonight. I am sure they will have told you about it already, Katie.'

'It's to celebrate the way your great-uncle returned to save the Antico estate in 1945, isn't it?'

'That's right.' Giovanni was gripped by a sudden impulse. 'Would you like to come?'

Her beautiful eyes became troubled. Giovanni cursed his reckless passion aboard the *Viola*. He had frightened her and lost her trust. Gazing at her now, he knew this chance to admire her might have to last him for the rest of his life. That thought forced him to play his trump card.

'I think perhaps you should, Katie. Think of it as a final opportunity to enjoy yourself before returning to real life.'

As he spoke, he glanced at the letter clutched in her hand.

'Does your mother expect you to bail her out by settling these bills?' he asked gently.

'Of course.'

'And will you?'

'It is called family loyalty,' Katie managed when she could force the words past the hard knot of indignation where her heart should be. 'What else can I do? Dad's health is not good, so I've told Mum she mustn't worry him. My mother has certain…problems when it comes to money. The result is that she looks to me to sort everything out for her.'

'I am no stranger to that type of person myself,' Giovanni said wearily. Once upon a time he had thought he was alone in working all the hours God sent for the benefit of someone else. It was horrible to discover he shared the experience—and with her, of all people.

'That is why my work is so important to me, Signor Amato. It allows me to fund the care my father needs—'

'—And your mother's spending,' he inserted grimly. 'Has she always been so reckless?' He gestured in the direction of the letter Katie was now running nervously through her fingers.

'I suppose so—she left home when I was young. Contact with her has been patchy for years. Still, I suppose she did me one favour. Growing up without her made me independent. My mother and I are totally unalike, Signor Amato. I don't need anyone in my life.'

A surge of pride gave him a sudden lift. 'That is not the message you sent out after my party on board the *Viola*. A cold-blooded woman would have shaken off my hands before I kissed her properly.'

She determinedly held back the tears that she could feel brewing. 'That was a lapse of professionalism, Signor. It will not happen again.'

With an awful finality, he nodded. 'I understand, but if you would still like to come to the party, my invitation stands. You can rest assured *I* will never add to your burden of worry again, Katie.'

Katie did not know which was the greater shock. The fact that Giovanni Amato now knew the grubby reality of her background, or that she had effectively slammed the door in the

face of the only man she would ever love. After their exchange
he had turned and gone straight back to work. She knew that
her only hope of seeing him again before she left for England
would be at the party that evening. At least she had a good
excuse to attend. He was, after all, her stellar client. The
example her mother set meant that money was always a worry
for Katie. She was careful with it, as she had seen what misery
debt could bring. After her father's heart surgery, she had
become doubly keen to provide financial security for him. As
a result, she could never fully relax before any payments
owing were safely lodged in the Carter Interiors bank account.
Worries about cash flow haunted her, and increased with her
mother's most recent plea for funds. Katie didn't want her
father stressed by his ex-wife's bills. She tried to believe that
it would be the last time, but things had fallen into a sadly pre-
dictable pattern. Katie would pay up, on the understanding
that the amount would be returned in monthly instalments.
These arrangements only ever lasted until her mother found
a rich new lover. Then she would be too busy to worry about
what she called 'minor details' like debt. Katie, and a growing
list of Mrs Carter's innocent new contacts, would be left to
wait for settlements that never happened.

   The last thing Katie needed to do was upset a client like
Giovanni Amato at a time when she was faced with the bills
for her mother's latest spending sprees.

Later, Katie met Eduardo as she was on her way down the
back stairs. When she mentioned her invitation to the party,
he warned her it was another black-tie affair. The same
thought struck them both at once. When he suggested in a
whisper that she might make use of a second dress from the
Contessa Lia's collection, they both knew which one it would

be. The green lamé might have been too daring for a charity dinner, but its stunning colour would strike exactly the right note at a party to celebrate the Antico estate's rebirth. As she showered and slipped into the beautiful bias-cut gown, Katie primed herself. Since arriving at the Villa Antico, she had discovered a new, slightly daring side to her personality. Tonight at the party she would give it free rein. Giovanni had accepted her first refusal as final, so she had nothing to lose. This evening she would hide her broken heart and try to forget her miserable, lonely future without him.

Remembering how Giovanni had reacted when she had hesitated at the top of his grand staircase, too scared to descend, Katie decided her attitude would be different from the start. This time she breezed out of her suite, head already held high. Then she got her first surprise. The usually quiet entrance hall was cheerful with chatter. She looked over the balustrade and saw all the house staff gathered below. They fell silent. As one, they all turned and gaped at her. Katie stopped. They stared. Only one person continued speaking. Giovanni Amato was still working, busy with his mobile phone. Then the outbreak of peace filtered through to him and he realised something had caught his employees' attention. As his call ended, he snapped the phone shut and turned to see what it was.

He stopped, looked up and rewarded her with a slow, lazy smile.

'Well, well, Miss Carter, you have done it again. You have pulled off another spectacular transformation.'

It was a reaction that filled Katie with confidence. She felt herself casting off the pain and growing in stature. It was not only because she wanted to act as though worthy of her surroundings. There was something about Giovanni's expression that drew her. He knew her guilty secrets, yet he could still look at her like that. Common sense told Katie that a real man like Giovanni must gaze at every woman like this, but she didn't have to believe it—not tonight.

'Get a move on, everybody—don't stand there like statues. We have a party to attend. Anyone would think you had never seen an English princess before.' He laughed, ushering his staff out through the great front doors.

Giggling, Katie hurried downstairs to join them. The train of her dress rippled after her, trickling over the steps like sparkling green water. For someone more used to the comfort and practicality of trousers, it was a wonderfully glamorous feeling. She carried herself now as she had done on that other fateful night. Unconsciously, she displayed all the qualities she was normally too shy to reveal in her client's presence.

By the time she reached the ground floor, everyone else had filed out. The place was deserted, with the notable exception of Giovanni Amato. He had been chivvying staff and gathering up his notes from a side table, but eventually he could not avoid turning his attention to his last guest.

When he turned and looked at her, Katie realised something. His face was alight in a way that made her feel weak with longing. He gazed at her for a long time, taking in everything from her pink painted toenails to the coils of red gold hair dressed around her shoulders. It was obvious he had something to say, but there was a long pause. Katie could only wait as good breeding fought with his instincts. He tapped the furl of papers he held in one hand against the palm of the other. He drew his lips tight against those perfect white teeth. All the time he maintained a dignified silence, until Katie could not stand it any longer.

'Do you think there is something wrong with this dress, Signor Amato?' she ventured.

'No...no, not at all.' His smile warmed her all over. 'If I am lost for words it is because I am realising what a treasure has been hidden under my own roof. You are a revelation to me, Katie. You are intelligent, you work hard and then you transform yourself like this.'

Katie laughed with him, but self-consciously. She had wound herself up to attend this party, but nothing had prepared her for his penetrating gaze. If only he had not said he would never repeat his approach on the *Viola*. Open admiration for her was written all over his face, but she knew a proud man like Giovanni would never go back on his word. She could only hope he could not read her mind. Chastity was the last thing he would find there.

He cleared his throat softly and spoke again. 'Katie, although I promised to keep things strictly impersonal between us tonight, I feel I must say something. Should you not be wearing jewellery to set off that dress?'

'I don't have any, Signor.'

'There was nothing wrong with the trinkets you wore on the *Viola*.'

'I can think of two things.' She giggled. Every movement rippled the chestnut tide of her hair into soft waves lapping over her creamy shoulders, he noticed.

'For one thing, blue jewellery doesn't exactly go with a green dress and, for another, those things were only borrowed.'

This inspired him. 'Then, if you don't mind, I shall lend you the perfect finishing touch for your ensemble. Wait there,' he commanded and went over to raid Eduardo's office. A few minutes later he emerged with a jingling collection of keys. Their rattle echoed through the great hall as he disappeared into the cavernous under-stairs area. Katie listened to the piping of electronics as he disabled a security system. She heard a heavy door open and his footsteps receded. An age later, all the sound effects were repeated in reverse order. He reappeared in the hall holding a flat leather case. Once the bunch of keys was safely returned to Eduardo's office, he strode over to a side table, which stood next to the cheval glass.

'Come here, Katie.'

She did as she was told.

'Now…turn around…'

He was busy behind her with the click of a fastening. Then she felt him draw very close. At the corner of her vision she saw his raised hands, before a cold glitter of diamonds and emeralds was dropped around her neck. Katie's hands went straight to the glorious waterfall of sparkling silver and green that ran from her throat to her cleavage.

The excitement of wearing real jewels was one thing. The physical thrill of having him so near and feeling his hands work their way beneath her hair to secure the necklace outshone it.

'I can't possibly wear this, Signor Amato!'

'Why not?' He was taking his time over the clasp. 'No one else makes use of them, and you can hardly attend the estate party dressed simply like that. You may prefer to put the earrings on yourself.'

Katie turned and saw a pair of elegant droplets exactly matching her borrowed necklace. They lay in a bed of black velvet, waiting to be loved. In seconds she had removed her plain gold sleepers and fixed the precious antiques in their place. When she looked in the cheval-glass, she gasped.

A generous smile toyed with Giovanni's features. He was standing back, evidently admiring the Amato jewels. Katie waited for him to say something. All he did was look at her—but his eyes were so eloquent, that was all it took. Desire for what might happen was almost crushed by fear of the consequences, but that did not stop her. In one quick movement she rose on tiptoe and touched a kiss against his cheek. He sprang back as though burned, but the moment passed so fast Katie was already halfway to the front door.

'Come on, Signor Amato—or they will start the party without you.'

It was a mistake, Giovanni thought. Everybody is enjoying themselves too much tonight—and that was the problem. *His* body was no exception—but it was his mind that really tortured him. His staff had goggled at the sight of an interior designer coming down that grand staircase dressed very like his late Contessa. That was bad enough, but it was nothing to the way they'd reacted on seeing her draped in Amato diamonds.

Dr Vittorio had been warning Giovanni about the dangers of overwork and isolation for years. Now it felt as if all his demons were finally catching up with him. His mind was not on the evening's noisy entertainment. He circulated, exchanging words with everyone, and accepted a glass of the Bacchari family's latest *tavola vino*. Small talk gave him the excuse to keep his eyes fixed firmly on his farmers and growers, rather than casting about the assembly and seeing Katie in *that* dress.

It was so like the one Lia had provoked him with that night—

He crushed the hideous thought and accepted another glass of wine. It was a first outing for this particular batch, Grandad Bacchari was telling him, which was drinkable without being a classic.

Giovanni hardly heard. He was lost in memory. Lia had known he disliked the colour green. It reminded him of unripe lemons, the hard, sour apples that grew wild around the estate—and jealousy. They had argued.

So what? That had been nothing new. Giovanni's lip curled with thoughts of life with his late Contessa. He obliged his tenants by sampling some more of their wine…and then a glitter at the edge of his vision made him turn his head.

It was Katie.

Giovanni remembered how the argument with Lia had begun. Dr Vittorio had been telling her for months that she did not need to lose any more weight, but she must have gone on dieting. In between her final fitting and the delivery of a consignment of gowns, Lia's measurements must have changed again. Giovanni had caught her padding out her new green dress with tissue and challenged her.

Their fight had been spectacular. Then Lia left him, in the middle of the night, and went home to her over-indulgent parents.

That felt like the end of everything, but a month later Lia returned. Then, things got much, much worse.

Giovanni had been alone for five years now. He had been freed from his cold, dead marriage—but by a disaster drawn straight from Dante's circles of hell.

He tried to focus on the party.

It was impossible. Katie was inspiring a drift of more recent happy memories. She obviously did not need to resort to tissue paper. Her dress fitted like a second skin. The gentle swell of her breasts rose above the boned, strapless bodice, appealing to every red-blooded male in the place. The jealousy he now recognised from that party on board the *Viola* struck again. Giovanni took another drink. He had been as sober as an inquisitor that night with Lia and it had done him no good at all.

It began to occur to him that the crowd around the wine-tasting table was thinning. People were moving off towards long trestle tables that had been set up at the far end of the marquee. As host, Giovanni waited until they sorted themselves out. Searching out Katie, he saw that she had found herself a seat. The Bacchari family had absorbed her into their clan. Then he made his way to the place of honour at the top table.

Giovanni cleared his throat. 'This is a very important evening for the Villa Antico estate,' he began, and every face turned to look at him. He was conscious of only one. He delivered a faultless speech of welcome and appreciation. As usual, it was crammed full of everything his audience wanted to hear. First, there were the old stories about everyone pitching in and doing their bit for the greater glory of the Amato family. Then, more recent events were highlighted, family by family. Finally, Giovanni rounded off his speech by talking about the future. Once again he managed to fit everything into the shortest possible time. As he always pointed out at the end, his tenants came to feast, not listen. This was greeted with a cheer and the eating began.

Giovanni was more than happy to let the gathering attack the food without him.

'Mmm…these calzone are good,' Dr Vittorio said through a healthy mouthful. 'I'm not so sure about the pasta salad, though. There are too many seeds in it for my liking. Gimi's eldest girl made it. She's on holiday from university, although I don't think Gimi is going to let the rest of his mob follow her there if they're all going to come back from Urbino as vegans—Oh, for goodness' sake!' the doctor burst out suddenly. 'Where are you, Giovanni? You certainly aren't here, listening to me!'

Giovanni roused himself, but without much enthusiasm for conversation. 'I have decided I don't like having house guests. They disrupt the place too much.'

'Oh, I suppose you're talking about your interior designer,' the doctor grunted into his dinner. 'Still, she won't be here for much longer, will she? I've heard she'll be gone by the weekend.'

'She is leaving tomorrow afternoon. Eduardo has already supervised her packing.'

'There you are, then.' The doctor hailed another passing calzone. 'In twenty-four hours' time you will be back to business as usual. She will be gone.'

'Leaving a trail of devastation in her wake,' Giovanni added.

CHAPTER SIX

KATIE was one OF the first to leave the celebration. She was also one of the last to get home. The Bacchari family invited her back to their farm and she had been unable to resist. The family's sow was due to give birth and they wanted to make sure the animal was not alone for the big event. Six people, including Katie, piled into an unstable old Fiat and clattered three kilometres to their holding. Nature had beaten them to it. Rosella the pig was already busy with half a dozen little ones by the time her audience arranged themselves around the low walls of her sty. Katie was treated to some home-cured salami and a drink that tasted as if it had been brewed from apricots and iron filings.

Eventually, young Pino was given the task of getting her back to the villa. This he did in record time, while Katie hung on with her fingertips and tried to keep smiling. The Fiat finally skittered to a halt outside the ancient walls of the original Antico enclosure. Katie got out and saw that Pino had parked beside a wooden door almost as old as the wall. When they finally wrestled it open, Katie realised she was entering the villa grounds by way of the swimming pool terrace. Beyond the illuminated stretch of water, the Villa Antico rose like a fortress. Only one light showed on its craggy stone face.

With a tingle of excitement, Katie realised it must be coming from Giovanni's suite. What was he doing in there? Just ordinary things, she told herself, but that didn't stop her wishing she could see him doing them. She watched for a moment, but there was no movement from within the bright, but closed, French windows. After saying goodbye to Pino, she started to cross the grass, but her feet were on fire. Taking off her borrowed sandals, she padded over to the pool in bare feet. There was no one about. No one would see.

Hoisting the beautiful green lamé dress up above her ankles, Katie stepped delicately on to the first level of the spray pool. The relief was wonderful. With a sigh, she sat down on the edge and dangled her feet into a deeper section. Sounds of the countryside at night stole over the high grey walls and into her sanctuary. Nightingales in the olive grove sang lullabies to cicadas and crickets out in the scrub. A warm breeze brought the fragrance of roses from climbers clothing the walls. It would be such a wrench to leave this place. Everything about the Villa Antico was so special. The people were wonderful, too.

And one person in particular, she admitted to herself. It was no use denying it. Work had always been her refuge from real life. Now things had changed. One word, one glance, from Giovanni Amato and work was no longer enough to satisfy her.

She would be leaving tomorrow afternoon. All they had shared was a few moments in moonlight, and only one proper kiss. Katie sighed again, imagining how it might have felt to give in and lose herself in his arms. If only she had not stopped herself responding to his kiss they might have been enjoying this evening together.

She sat up straight, telling herself she was being ridiculous. Fantasising about Giovanni tonight did not help, any more than

it had done over the past few weeks. Why he managed to cast
such a spell over her was a mystery. The man was a total work-
aholic. As a count, he probably took little notice of ordinary
people like her, and he certainly didn't grant wishes. And yet...

Katie knew she had to be firm with herself. There was no
point in wasting any time on affairs of the heart. People
messed you around and let you down. Work never did that. You
got out of it what you put in. Katie was a firm believer in the
old saying that the more you gave, the better it got. And yet...

She could not bear to let herself think back to that single
time aboard the *Viola*. It was torture enough remembering
how it had felt to kiss his cheek in the entrance hall earlier.
His skin had been smooth and warm. If she tried hard, she
could still taste the cedary, spicy tang of his aftershave.

As she recalled the sensations, her lips burned with those
memories from the yacht. It had started with such an innocent
gesture. Then her emotions had been fired in a way she had
never experienced before. When he had gone on to possess her
lips with such urgency, she had been brought to fever pitch.

Katie closed her eyes, reliving the moment. On the other
side of the wall a new nightingale began its recital. She lay
back on the smooth, flat stones of the pool surround. They
were still warm from the day's intense heat, but a chill ran
through her as she heard an unexpected sound. The grating
of a lock cut all the birdsong off in mid-flow. She sat up.
Someone had opened the French windows of the illuminated
suite above her. They were walking out on to its balcony.
That someone could only be seen in silhouette, but Katie
knew who it was. No one but Giovanni Amato had such an
aura of silent power. Nothing moved. Beyond his garden wall,
even nature fell silent.

Katie's hand flew to her neck.

'It is no use trying to hide, Katie.' His voice was low with amusement. 'You are twinkling like Venice across the lagoon.'

'I didn't want to keep the necklace and earrings on after the party, Signor Amato—I asked Eduardo to take them back before I went off with the Bacchari family. He said only you were allowed to take them.' She was gabbling, suddenly aware of the risk she had run with his heirlooms. 'I was very careful, and the Bacchari are all *very* honest.'

'Calm down—nothing has happened to them, has it? In any case, I was rather more concerned about you. If they take a liking to someone, the Bacchari can be overwhelming. I sent Raphael down to the farm in case you needed an excuse to escape from them.'

Katie scrambled to her feet. 'Then I'm afraid he's had a wasted journey.' Picking up her shoes, she began to head in the direction of the villa's front door. When she reached it a few minutes later, Giovanni opened it himself.

'Oh, no. I suppose you had to open the door because Raphael is out looking for me!' Her guilt increased by the second as she followed Giovanni into the house.

'Don't worry—it is nothing. I would have come down in any case, to relieve you of the jewellery.'

She went over to the side table where the battered leather case still lay open. The only things lying on its worn black velvet were her small gold ear studs. She laid the emerald and diamond droplets down in their tailor-made indentations and put her own earrings back in. Then she bundled the luxuriance of her hair up on to the top of her head so that he could unfasten the necklace.

It was no easier for Giovanni's hands the second time he attacked the problem. Despite that, he kept any contact between his fingers and her skin to a minimum. The nearness of him fanned the flame of desire that had been dancing deep inside Katie since their very first kiss. She tried leaning back towards him, but the treacherous necklace was already slipping away, drawn on to his palm for inspection. Katie let down her hair, ruffling it into position over her bare shoulders again.

'There's nothing wrong with it, is there?' she asked with concern as he continued to run the fine, warm gold through his fingers.

'No, nothing at all.' He moved to lay the precious antique back in its velvet bed. This he managed without fully turning his back on her. She moved her bare feet on the cold tiles of the hall. This provided wonderful relief for her sore toes, but it did not prompt Giovanni into giving her any clues about whether she should retreat to her room.

'Thank you for inviting me this evening, Signor Amato.'

'Think nothing of it.'

He was concentrating on closing the jewellery case. As he moved, she caught the warm aroma of him again. His after-shave was fainter now, and tinged with the ghostly essence of party. Katie knew time was running out for her.

'I really enjoyed myself, Signor.'

'Despite the fact that you spent half the evening in a farmyard?'

There was no hiding the amusement in his voice. With a heavy heart, Katie came to the conclusion she had been dreading. An aristocrat like Giovanni was not going to give her a second chance to snub him. She might as well give up all her romantic dreams now, before she made a complete fool of herself. With regret, she lifted the hem of her skirt and set off up the grand stair-case. It was only when she reached the top that she realised no sound of doors, keys or security systems was reaching her from down in the hall. Instinctively, she stopped and looked back.

Giovanni had not moved from his position beside the table, but something had changed. He was watching her. Katie pulled herself up to her full height and returned his gaze with equal openness. She was not going to let him think she was in any way disappointed about anything. Independence had got her this far in life. It would see her through the pain of crushed fantasies.

'Goodnight, Signor Amato.'

He gave a nod of acknowledgement. 'Goodnight, Katie.'

There was nothing that could possibly be read from his expression. With a hollow heart, Katie continued to her rooms.

She hardly had time to put down her sandals before there was a light tap on the main door of her suite. She jumped and, hurrying through from her dressing room, stopped a metre short of the door to listen. There was no sound from outside. Perhaps it had been her imagination. For ten heartbeats she waited. Then the silence was broken by another knock, louder this time. It took a few seconds for Katie to find her voice. All the time her mind was working frantically. *If it is Giovanni, he will not wait,* she thought. *He will go away, and I shall be saved from any more shame.*

The knock came again.

Katie tried to fool herself that it could not possibly be him. It could *not* be, after all this delay.

'Who is it?'

'Me.'

Her heart bounced so hard against her ribs that she could not catch her breath.

'What do you want?' she gasped, praying that she did not know the answer, but hoping that she did.

'I forgot to offer you coffee. Some was prepared for me, if you would like to take advantage of it.'

It was the chance of seeing him again, not coffee, that persuaded Katie to unlock her door. He had taken off his jacket and waistcoat, but looked as magnificent as ever. Outlined by soft light from the hallway, he held out a thimble-sized cup of espresso. It sat on a bone china saucer, dwarfed by his hand. His perfect, pale gold skin contrasted with the stark white of his turned back shirtsleeves. Katie looked up at him. His expression was as enigmatic as ever. If there was any question in his mind, he was going to make *her* put it into words.

She reached out to take the coffee from him.

'Thank you, Signor Amato.'

He inclined his head slightly. 'You are welcome, Katie.'

'Well, this should make sure neither of us sleeps tonight.'

She meant it innocently enough, but it had the effect of making them look at each other warily. Katie took a step back into her suite. Giovanni started to leave, then thought of something and turned back. 'That reminds me—I might have to go into the office first thing, Katie. This may be the last time we speak before you leave. I have no doubt your stay here will have been successful, but I should like to wish you a good journey home.' His mouth twitched in a formal smile. Katie took it to mean that her audience was at an end. All she had to do was bring things to a dignified close.

'Then I must thank you again, Signor Amato. As I mentioned before, I have really enjoyed my stay here.' Her smile was equally brief, but genuine. Especially when she thought of the touch of his lips against her own… 'I will be in touch in due course. Goodnight.'

It took all Katie's will-power to close the door on him. She stood, leaning back against it, until his footsteps faded away along the hall outside. She should have known better than to expect a man like that to wait for her to change her mind.

* * *

She had missed her last chance. Katie went over to her dining table and sat down. There was nothing else left for her to do but drink the coffee. She lifted the cup he had given her. Its contents were as thick and black as molasses, but not as sweet. The saucer held a spoon, but no sugar. She looked down into the depths of his favourite Napoli blend. Its oil-dark surface trembled with concentric rings, throbbing in time to her pulse.

Nobody could be expected to drink this without sugar. Grabbing the opportunity, Katie flung open her door and walked along the corridor to Giovanni's suite.

She heard the ancient floorboards creaking long before he eventually opened the door. Wall lights dimly illuminated his room and a soft resinous sigh of cedar wood and coffee drifted out to meet her.

'Katie?' he enquired as though it was the first time they had met that day. 'Can I do something more for you?'

'Yes! That is…I—I mean, may I have some sugar for my coffee, please?'

'I'm sorry, I don't use it.' His grey eyes had already lost their thoughtfulness. They were now questioning her closely. 'And neither do you.'

'I do when I drink espresso,' she improvised a shade defensively.

'There may be some milk in my fridge,' he said carefully. 'Eduardo keeps it well stocked, but I don't often drink *latte* in here.'

'In your fridge,' Katie repeated faintly. 'Right.'

They continued to look at each other for some time, until he stood back and gave her a prompt. 'Would you like to come in and get some?'

She looked up at him tentatively 'Yes. '

He took another step back to allow her in. Katie walked

forward and then jumped like a frog at the sound of a soft click. Looking over her shoulder, she saw that he had closed the door.

'Would you prefer me to leave it open, Katie?'

'No—no, not at all.'

He led the way, one hand placed protectively on the small of her back to guide her.

She took one last look around his drawing room as she went with him. In the course of her work she had been over every inch of it and the plans of his entire suite were safely stored in her luggage. But that was not real. There was no substitute for inhaling the rich masculinity of his natural surroundings, or feeling the hard-packed luxury of genuine Turkish rugs beneath her toes.

'I'm glad you called. Are your French windows open?' His rich, deep voice drifted over her and his soft touch made her shiver.

'No, I closed them before we left for the party.'

'That's a pity. I was going to suggest you take this last drink of the evening as I do, to the accompaniment of the nightingales outside. The noise of your doors being unlocked is sure to disturb them. They are in full flow now—can you hear?'

She nodded.

'Why don't you come and share my table and listen to them from there?'

Katie could not wait. This was her last night at the Villa Antico. Her one remaining chance to share some time alone with this man who dominated her every waking moment and her dreams as well.

As she nodded, he poured a thin stream of creamy milk into her cup, watching for her signal to stop.

'That's enough.' She sensed him putting the container back

and closing the door, but could not look. He did not offer her another direct invitation to join him. Instead he went to stand beside a small table in his salon. It was set up just inside his open French windows and, as she approached Katie enjoyed the liquid cadences of half a dozen nightingales rippling in from the night.

A single chair stood beside the table, which Giovanni pulled out. Swinging a matching antique seat over from its place beside the wall, he sat down beside her. The table was so small that beneath its surface she could sense the nearness of him. She would have loved to lose herself in the nightingales' song, but the distraction of having such a man within touching distance filled her mind. She had been finding it difficult to look at him directly, ever since that moment on the boat. Now her heart trembled each time she heard his coffee spoon rattle against its saucer or caught sight of his hand as he reached for one of the biscotti lying on a plate in the centre of the table. Her silence did nothing to disturb him. In fact, he seemed more at ease than when they had been downstairs in the hall together.

'I should tell you that I don't make a habit of visiting strange men after dark, Signor Amato,' she managed, whispering for the sake of the birdsong.

'I have never considered myself to be strange. In fact, for many years I was the only normal person I knew. Now *you* are unfathomable, Katie. For example, you dress like a duchess for a trip to a pigsty.'

She looked up at him quickly and saw that he was smiling. She smiled, too.

'That's better. You have had a haunted look about you for days, Katie.' He fell silent again, but she felt that the tension between them had eased slightly. As a result she relaxed and managed to take some pleasure in the natural cadences throbbing in through the window.

The sound of a distant engine grew closer and became the rattle of a farm vehicle. Their nightingales shivered into silence. The racket out in the lane bucked and kicked all the way along the other side of the terrace wall. As the vehicle passed by, its engine note changed. They heard it check, reverse and then stop altogether. After that performance, the only sound left was a far off owl, hunting along the river valley. Katie clicked her tongue in disappointment that there would be no more nightingales, at least for a while.

'That is Raphael, returning from his search for you.' Giovanni drained his coffee. Putting down the cup, he began going through the pockets of the jacket hanging from his chair.

Katie stood up. 'I must go. Raphael will need to come and tell you that I put him to a lot of trouble for nothing,' she began, but Giovanni motioned for her to stop while he used his mobile. Opening it, he pressed a few buttons, then smiled into the middle distance as it was answered.

'Raphael? *Si, so. Grazie e buona notte,* Raphael.'

He snapped the phone shut with a flourish. 'There. That has ensured we will not be disturbed again. Raphael will be halfway to Elena's arms by now.'

Any concern for her own safety vanished as Katie realised the staff might have more to worry about than she did.

'You aren't supposed to know about *that*!' she said desperately. Elena had told her about the romance in giggling confidence. The girl had been horrified at the thought her employer might find out. Giovanni's only reaction to the news was to twitch a shoulder dismissively.

'Relationships between unmarried servants was almost a

hanging offence in my great-uncle's day, but I take a more…liberal stance.'

Katie breathed again. 'Oh, Raphael and Elena will be so glad to hear that.'

He inhaled deeply. 'Actually, I'd be grateful if you kept my admission to yourself. I like to keep them on their toes.'

She smiled. 'Of course, Signor, which is why I must go now, to show them that you play by the same rules.'

'Ah.' He stood up, a lazy, teasing smile forming on his lips. 'That need not necessarily be true, Katie.'

She waited, hardly daring to breathe. He took two slow, measured steps towards her. 'You look exquisite tonight. And you know, as well as I do, what happened the last time I saw you looking so beautiful.'

'I haven't been able to forget it like you.' It was meant as a rebuke, but she realised as soon as she spoke that he read it quite differently. His bittersweet smile touched her through the shadows and from that moment on she was lost.

'Oh, Katie, if you can read my mind like that, why have you been so distant since that night on the *Viola*? If I frightened you then by going too fast, it was only because I found you so irresistible.'

She gasped, wondering how to tell him how tortured she had been. There was no need. He took her gently in his arms and sipped a single gentle kiss from her lips.

'Oh, Giovanni…' she breathed. All thoughts of his other women vanished with the realisation he was going to give her a second chance. Katie had spent every moment since the *Viola* regretting the way she had recoiled from him. Tonight was going to be different.

Dimly, far off, the sounds of nightingales began drifting in through the open windows again. Giovanni barely heard them.

His senses were full of the steady, insistent beat of life, rising with an intensity he had never enjoyed before. He moved one hand to her hair, caressing it away from the silken skin of her shoulders. Then he dipped his head to sample the taste of her. It was more delicious than he had imagined, and he had imagined it often. His hands slid to her waist, holding her protectively as he kissed her again and again. This was wonderful, and her gentle modesty was so refreshing. It had been a fact of life since Giovanni's teens that women threw themselves at him. They flirted, they cajoled, they stripped and jiggled. The only woman who had done nothing for him was Lia.

He pondered this thought as he stood in the half dark with Katie in his arms. Lia had been ice—except when wearing that green dress, so like this one—then she had become a spitting, vicious fury. In contrast, Katie was like orchid petals beneath his hands.

For once, he shut his mind to memory. This was so much more restful. Katie showed no signs of nagging him for anything, and holding her was giving him so much pleasure. Surely she deserved something in reward?

After some long and deliciously stress-free moments, she received what she had been yearning for.

CHAPTER SEVEN

GIOVANNI bent forward and rested his face against the side of hers, breathing in the perfume of clean hair and warm skin. He could afford to take his time. Usually, there were so many calls on him that an unspoken urgency to get on, to get busy, to get going drove him on. Tonight was different. There was no hurry, especially as the full-on approach had scared her away before. He nuzzled her neck, searching for the right spot. Every woman had one, and this alabaster figurine was no different. With a soft moan her head fell back, exposing her throat. Kissing and nibbling his way up to her lips, he cradled her close to his body. His hands strayed down to cup her bottom, gently kneading it, as he tasted her lips properly for the first time. She responded. This was infinitely better than his impulsive approach on the *Viola*. With a rush of satisfaction, he felt his kiss returned. His own response was increased a million times by knowing that he was fuelling a growing desire within her. She was eager for him this time. He relished the way her mouth accepted the first tentative touch of his tongue tip. When her arms wound around his neck as though she would never let him go, it told him everything he wanted to know. That realisation, coupled with his growing physical arousal, was a turning point. He seized the opportunity in both hands. This woman had fascinated him since the first moment she had arrived in his office. She had charmed his staff, his relations and his business associates. Now it was his turn.

Katie was beautiful; she was everything he could wish for in a woman and, best of all, she was foreign and a contractor. He could take her tonight without any of the society harpies who craved his body being any the wiser. Katie's discretion was legendary. Tonight's enjoyment would be theirs alone. It would be sex pure and simple, with no questions asked and no comeback.

The idea inflamed him. Working his hands inside her dress, he felt the delicacy of lace panties beneath his fingers. She trembled as he eased her out of her clothes, but she never protested. Her lips were too hungry for him.

'You want me.'

His low, urgent voice contained all the desire Katie recognised in herself. She thrilled with the vibration of it. His maleness was raw, total and so completely irresistible. When he kissed her now, his urgency was almost out of control. There could be no going back—and she did not want to. Passion powered her until she felt dizzy.

He took her mouth, his tongue thrusting demands that were answered by her faint mews of delight. That was all the encouragement he needed. It set his hands roaming over her body again, testing each curve and nuance of her nakedness. A long, low moan of pleasure escaped from Katie's lips as he crushed her body against his own. With a need born of instinct, she pushed her hips against him, mirroring his own movements.

'Bed is the only place for this,' he murmured and was not to be denied. She had tempted him for so long. It was time to do something about it. Burying his face against her shoulder, he lifted her off the ground and carried her into his shadowy room. Settling her gently on the bed, he lay down beside her, fully clothed. Supporting his head with one hand, he used the other to appreciate the smooth rise and fall of her body.

He breathed in the warm perfume of her hair again. Her fingers responded, tentatively at first, then with more certainty as they found buttons. With his encouragement she undid them, one by one. Dragging off his shirt, he pulled her closer still. The sensation of his crisp curls of chest hair pressed against her tender flesh squeezed out a ragged gasp of anticipation.

'You enjoy the touch of skin against skin?'

She could hear the smile in his voice as his hand circled her shoulder and then swooped down to cup her breast. Each finger moved independently, bringing her nipple to sharp arousal before going anywhere near it. When at last his thumb rolled over the dark bead, its pad raised her effortlessly to a peak of excitement. He kissed her again, his tongue exploring her willing depths as his fingers continued to tease her breast. Then, slowly but surely, he kissed his way down over her cheek, her neck and the delicate collar-bones he had so admired at the party. When she offered no resistance he moved lower, until his playful hand slipped away to her ribcage.

As taut as a violin string, Katie waited. She could feel his breath dancing over her skin. Then tiny kisses rained down on her, circling the proud summit of her nipple until she could stand it no more. Closing her hands around his head, she drew his mouth towards her breast. It had the desired effect. His body rose up, rolling her on to her back. His mouth enveloped her nipple while his chest pressed against her nakedness. The light pressure of his body on hers was maintained as the tip of his tongue teased spasm after spasm of excitement from her. All the while he was stroking the roughness of his chest hair against the delicate skin of her belly. Rhythmic movements crushed his lower body against her legs. She could feel the hardness of him, even though it was still contained within his clothes.

Katie was beyond imagining. She wanted to unleash all his power, to absorb it greedily and take everything from him that she had so far denied herself. In his bed there could be no fear of rejection, only a desperate need to accept everything he was offering to her. Her body reacted to him instinctively, primitive urges driving her higher and higher. Her back arched, her hair tangled against his white pillows and she became aware of a strange song crying through the night. It took a while to realise she was responsible for the sound. He was bringing a whole new, wordless language to her lips. She was hardly conscious of anything but his delight as he revelled in her reactions.

Giovanni was still determined to make all the rules. Taking his time like the connoisseur he was, he moved kiss by kiss across her. The pleasure repeated was more than redoubled. Once again, he savoured the feel of her beneath his fingers and lips. She was so responsive. The more she enjoyed herself, the more he wanted to prolong the satisfaction it gave him. Despite that, the warm night and the extent of his physical arousal were making clothes too restricting. He stopped caressing the sensitive skin beneath her arm for a moment and released the buckle of his belt. She froze at the sound. He paused.

'What is the matter?'

'Nothing. Nothing at all.'

There was a certainty in her voice that made him wonder. He rolled away from her and sat up. She did not move.

'There is enough trouble in the world already without an unwilling partner in bed.' He looked across at her intently. 'Do you want me to carry on?'

Katie held her breath and tried to catch her thoughts. She wanted this more than anything else in the world. It was so wrong and yet so right. All her life she had fought against letting anyone get too close. Now none of that seemed to matter. She was suspended in a dream, desperate for the simple human contact she had denied herself for so long. And what a way to indulge her desires. The sight of his naked body in the swimming pool had been electrifying enough. Now it was warm and available on the bed beside her. She wanted to touch, explore, enjoy…Was that such a crime?

Soundlessly she sat up and reached for him. Neither of them needed any more encouragement. His mouth searched hungrily for hers and possessed it. As they sank down on to the bed again, her hands roamed over his smooth back. Undulating beneath her hands, he eased his way out of the rest of his clothes until they were both free to explore through the anonymity of night.

Katie had never known such abandon. His body felt as good as it looked. Biceps toned and sleek from exercise and the smooth hard curves of his chest were all hers to fondle. As he kissed her, she searched for his nipples. They were as hard as hers. She tried to copy the movements he had used to kindle fire in her. Instead of enjoying it as she had anticipated, he convulsed, catching at her hands.

'That is too much of the wrong sort of pleasure,' he whispered, his laughter liquid in the shadows. Taking her hand, he returned it to the small of his back.

It had never occurred to her that men could be ticklish. She wondered what other parts of his body might be open to exploration. Bewitched by his kisses, she let her hands stray forward over the rise of his hip. He did not stop her this time. Instead he twisted his body so that her fingers could find what they were seeking. She gasped. The combination of sensitivity and thrusting maleness fascinated her. Encircling him with her touch, she felt his arousal kick with anticipation. Trying to catch a glimpse of him through the darkness, she leaned forward. As she did so, a lock of her hair coiled against his thighs.

He responded gruffly. 'I was concentrating on *you*.'

Rolling her over again, he moved his hands appreciatively until he reached the cap of curls that hid her sex. His palm covered it for a moment, the fingers resting lightly on her thighs. Katie could not help herself. When his fingertips asked a silent question, her body replied. He parted her petals and found nectar. By coaxing the tiny bud at the heart of her femininity, his expertise sent her into ecstasy overload.

Katie had not known such perfection was possible. It was incredible and almost too much to bear. He was sending fervent darts of excitement so deep into her that they began to cross the line between pleasure and pain. She writhed around to catch him again, grasping the shaft that pulsed so magnificently between her hands.

'This is supposed to be for your benefit, not mine.' His thick chuckle reached her through a miasma of need.

'It will be.' She sighed as her fingertips explored the beauty she had imagined so often. With delight, she recognised a sudden wicked urge to kiss and nibble all the places that were reacting so vividly beneath her touch. 'This is better than I could ever have imagined, Giovanni.'

He gave a wicked smile. 'And this is only a warm up to the main event.' Stretching out on the bed, he wondered why tonight should be so unusual. He felt strangely light-hearted for once. Whether it was the Baccharis' *vino*, the lateness of the hour or…something else, there was a subtle difference in this evening's pleasure. Katie had a distinctive way about her, that was for sure. Most women only wanted to take pleasure from his hands and mouth. She was different. She wanted to give as well, and continually whispered to him for instructions. She had a mischievous hesitancy—but surely no woman he bedded could be *that* innocent. It could have provoked him. It wouldn't have been the first time he unmasked a woman for acting a part, clamouring for his money and status. Instead, Katie aroused something more than lust in him—curiosity, for one thing. She had spent virtually her whole stay at the Villa Antico dressed in camouflage, with her head down and working busily. Only on two occasions had she emerged, like a butterfly from a chrysalis. Each time something had inspired him to act out of character. First, he had kissed her. And now he was going much, much further. What on earth was it about this woman that moved him to do such things?

There was no need to ask what was happening at the moment. Katie was using her beautiful mouth in most enjoyable ways. He smiled and shut his eyes, thinking of his latest harbour bill for the *Viola* in an attempt to quell the rising tide of his urgency. After a few moments he gave up. She was so good, so distracting that going all the way with her began to feel like the worst idea in the history of big mistakes. For five years, Giovanni had stubbornly refused to allow any woman to have influence over him. Katie could easily smash that rule. Making love to her once would not be enough. He knew he would need to repeat the experience with her, and her alone; over and over again…so he had to call a halt now, before things went too far.

He drew her up towards him. 'No more of that for the moment, Katie.'

'Oh, but I was enjoying it,' she breathed.

Kissing her deeply, he replied, 'This evening is about giving you pleasure.'

'But what about *you*?' she whispered.

'Tonight, Katie, all I'm interested in is *your* enjoyment.'

She looked up at him in puzzled innocence. 'That doesn't sound very satisfying for you.'

'It's fine,' he murmured, stroking her face.

But she drew away from him. 'So…don't you want me after all?'

Her voice was very small. She sounded so vulnerable, so innocent. He reached down and lifted her up until they were face to face. Then he began kissing the inquisitiveness out of her.

She responded by straddling his body and he could feel that glorious tumble of hair rippling over his own skin as he pressed his mouth against hers again. With senses heightened, he could feel the very personal imprint of her against his hard, flat belly. Wrapping his arms around her waist, he bundled her over on to her back He had intended to overwhelm her with pleasure again, without giving her the chance to raise questions in his own mind. Her reaction got the better of him. It was purely physical. Twining her limbs around him, she pleaded with her body.

He hovered between sense and desire. The fact that she was a temporary attraction spurred him on. After all—where would be the harm? Tomorrow she would be gone.

He sighed and in response she breathed his name softly into the night.

'Are you safe?' he questioned.

'Oh, yes…perfectly…please…take me…'

Her soft entreaty would have been hard enough to refuse. When her hands went up to cup his face in appeal, it broke the final link in the chain of his self-control. In a torment of ecstasy he plunged into her. At the exact moment when he realised why she was so different from all his other women she cried out.

'You were a virgin?' Heart pounding, he forced the words into the night.

She could not reply and he could not repeat the question. Giovanni cursed himself again for being overtaken by events. This should not be happening. Horror at the responsibility of being her first lover struggled inside him with primal male delight at being the only one to possess such purity. They lay perfectly still, their two hearts thundering as one. Then, in the same instant, both began to move. Ebb and flow, together and apart. Slow, perfectly synchronised movements drew them towards an experience that neither would ever forget. It felt as though no one in the history of the world had experienced such totally absorbing delight. For eternity and for no time at all they were locked in an embrace that could have only one conclusion. As she felt him begin to pulse with ecstasy, she kissed him as though with her dying breath. In one last unbearable pang of longing he exploded, driving his passion deep within her. He had found satisfaction. This was it. This was what he had been searching for, for so long…

Later, much later, night crowded in on them again. Giovanni's hold on her became a caress as he rolled on to his side, drawing her with him.

'You may not have come here to audition for the role of mistress, Katie, but believe me, it's yours. Any time you want it,' he murmured deep into her ear.

She listened to the steady rise and fall of his breathing, so different from her own ragged gasps. Her limbs were trembling from the powerful reactions he had fuelled in her, over and over again. It was not only physical feelings that tormented her now, but also realisation. Giovanni had made her his contessa for the evening, but he considered her to be nothing more than mistress material. He had just said as much. She had allowed herself one night of passion, but now knew that the experience could never be repeated. This was a man who had been unable to find love, although every rich and titled woman in the world had been paraded for his approval. There was only one reason why he had taken her to bed tonight, and it was not affection. Lust had driven her, too, but there was also a deeper undercurrent. Now, in darkness, she realised what it was. She loved him with a fervour that was painful. This had been her fairy tale, where the handsome prince transformed her with words that really meant something. But the truth was that there could be no happy ever after. The morning would divide them for ever. Giovanni would go back to his world and she must return to hers.

A single tear escaped from the corner of her eye. Tonight had been paradise. It was also everything she feared most in the entire world. She had let him into her mind and from there, into her body. For one brief, shining moment Katie had believed it could be for ever. Now, in the blank, sleepless hours before dawn all she could think of was her childhood. She had always tried to do everything right. Her mother had soaked up all her love, but had abandoned her when something better had come along. Katie knew that if she tried to stay with Giovanni, the same thing would happen. He would cast her off—if not today, then tomorrow or the next… History would repeat itself, magnifying her pain.

She had to get away now, before it was too late.

Giovanni's brow was pressed against her own as his arm encircled her. It was a weight she would have been only too happy to bear if it had come alone. Instead, it held all the horrors of the past. She loved him, so he would leave her. That was how loving had always worked in her life so far. Katie could not expect Giovanni to be any different.

He pulled her closer, fitting her snugly against his body.

It was not enough. She had to escape—she had to get away before he could trample on her heart.

CHAPTER EIGHT

A LOUD banging wakened Giovanni next morning. Gradually, he realised it was not only going on inside his head. Somebody was knocking at the door of his suite. He rolled into a sitting position and found that Katie was missing.

'Come in,' he called out, wincing. It was dazzlingly bright. Late mornings never did him any good. He reached for his watch, but it must have stopped the evening before. The display showed eight forty-five.

The door opened, but it was not Katie. It was Eduardo, carrying a tray and a sheaf of correspondence.

'Good morning, Signor. Here is your breakfast and I have printed out the emails received so far this morning.'

Giovanni checked his Rolex again. 'Then I really have overslept?'

'Indeed, Signor.'

Groaning, he rubbed his face. He needed a shave.

'Did everyone have a good time last night, Eduardo?' he began casually.

There was a significant pause. 'Yes, sir.'

'It was a good evening, although the Baccharis' latest *vino* ought to have a health warning on it.'

As he spoke he remembered his night tray and groaned

again. It was still standing on the table, complete with the telltale wreckage of two empty cups.

'Perhaps I should tell you at this point that Miss Carter has already left for Malpensa, Signor.'

'Katie has gone?' Giovanni gasped.

'Indeed, sir. In her eagerness to get away, the young lady apparently *carried her own cases downstairs*.' Eduardo was tight-lipped with disapproval at such a break with tradition. 'Nonna Bacchari was on her way to work in the kitchens and she saw the taxi arrive.'

Giovanni leaned forward and rubbed a weary hand through his hair. Of course she had gone. He had seduced her—a virgin. 'Mistress' was obviously not the word she wanted to hear. He groaned. Not even Katie could sleep with him without hearing wedding bells. Women really were all the same. Why had he expected anything else from her?

Eduardo swept around his employer's king-sized bed, but hesitated before actually picking up the abandoned coffee cups.

'Shall I close the windows, Signor?'

They had been left standing open all night. Giovanni stared into the cup of espresso he was holding. It stared back at him, as black as his thoughts.

'Do you know what went on in here last night, Eduardo?' he said slowly.

Eduardo looked at him directly for the first time that morning. The PA wore a particularly wintry expression as he cleared his throat to reply. 'I really have no idea, Signor. And neither do the rest of the staff. That is none of our business.'

Partly satisfied, Giovanni turned his attention to breakfast. He could rely on his staff to be discreet. His own conscience was more of a problem. Sex with Lia—it could never have been called 'making love'—had shown him what a dangerous activity it could be. At best it was nothing but a bargaining tool, at worst, a death sentence. And now he had risked everything with Katie. The girl whose uncomplicated loveliness promised everything had proved to be interested only in status, like all the rest.

Abandoning the breakfast, he realised there was only one way to wipe all this from the record. He would have to plunge into the day and get working.

Katie ran. She arrived at Milan Airport hours before her plane was due to leave for England. There would have been plenty of time to go right into the city, roam the Via Montenapoleone or call in to the Café Doney. Instead, she sat beside her cases on the concourse and waited. Her mobile rang constantly, but it was only work. A million people passed her by, but the million and first never arrived to carry her back to his villa.

There was no point in asking herself what she had done. That was only too apparent, from the dull ache, the vacancy, where she had held him so close for such a perfect time. It was obvious, too, from the way she was the only woman wearing a jacket on that hot day. Her fingers strayed beneath its fabric to the bruises made by Giovanni's teeth. She had thought she was alone in experiencing such ecstasy. Then she had felt all her own feelings mirrored in Giovanni's rapture, each time they had made love. It had been spectacular.

Now it was over. She could never see him again. Katie knew she was deluding herself by expecting him to rush to the airport and stop her flight. They were complete opposites in every way. He could never love her. He had said as much, in the way he had offered her the job of mistress. She doubted that Giovanni could love anyone. Aristocrats could afford to turn their backs on their conquests. Katie had suffered abandonment once and was not about to let it happen again. So she was going to make it simple for them both by leaving him before he could dump her. She would slip back into real life. From now on her staff could deal with the fantasy that was the Villa Antico.

Katie's success at the charity party on board the *Viola* paid dividends. Carter Interiors suddenly had more work than any normal company of its size could handle, but they managed magnificently. Katie worked eighteen-hour days, but for all the wrong reasons. Once it would have been for the love of it. Now it was to block out the pain that was coming at her from all directions. It was not only Giovanni who was breaking her heart. After exhausting the patience of her current lover, Mrs Carter had moved back home permanently. Katie worried about her father all the time. He was still unwell and she could not bear to see the hope in his eyes. He was trying to convince himself that his ex-wife had returned for good, but Katie knew better. Her mother would be off again, as soon as there was more generosity on offer elsewhere. Until that time, she expected to be waited on as a guest. Katie had no problem in looking after her dad, but her mother was entirely different. Nothing was ever right: the TV was the wrong size, the kitchen was five years out of date and the patterned carpets gave her a migraine. Katie coped by practically living in her office, or out on jobs. Both she and her father lost weight. Mrs Carter never cooked and, after years of Katie's good home baking, Mr Carter found it hard to tolerate ready meals and takeaway food.

Katie was often too busy to eat. Her tastes had changed since returning from Italy as well. The smell of milk in her tea now turned her stomach. Fried food of any sort made her long for the cooking of the Villa Antico. She was living mainly on pasta and fruit. It was a hollow attempt to relive those few unforgettable weeks.

She knew she should delegate the rest of the Villa Antico job. Each time she checked the wall chart of work in progress, the gold star signifying the date of a confirmation visit drew her eyes. *Someone* would have to go to Tuscany with the final plans and samples. Could she risk one of the girls? Or would Giovanni Amato ensnare her, too? Katie could not bear to think of anybody else sharing her sentence of checking emails hourly and snatching at ringing telephones.

She wondered about sending one of the guys—although that could be worse. He might come back with lurid tales of what Giovanni was getting up to and with whom. Katie did not want to find out things like that at second-hand. Her mind was full of suspicion already.

Finally the day came when a decision had to be made. Katie spent a sleepless night. She began by turning over in her mind the dangers of sending someone else. Then she added up the advantages of going herself. She already knew how plausible Giovanni Amato's charm was. This time she would be immune to it. She pushed her secret desire to see him again to the back of her mind, convincing herself that it was the best thing for the company if she went herself.

It was nearly two a.m. when Katie finally rolled over to try and settle down. As she did so, she winced. All the weight she was losing seemed to be migrating to her breasts. Making a sleepy note to buy some new bras for her trip to Tuscany, she closed her eyes and drifted off to sleep.

* * *

It had been warm during her first visit. Now it was intol-
erably hot. The sun hit with the force of a hammer, baking
stones and pedestrians alike. Katie was relieved to see a Villa
Antico chauffeur waiting for her at the airport as arranged. She
almost forgot her nervousness as he swung her cases into the
limousine that had been sent to collect her. All she had to do
was sink into its air-conditioned luxury.

'Signor Amato sends his apologies but he will not be at the
villa when you arrive, Miss Carter.' Her driver threw the information over his shoulder as he eased the big car out on to
the busy road.

'Thank you, Sebastien.' Katie smiled but her thoughts were
jumbled. She might just as well have sent someone from the
office after all. It would have saved her all this tiresome travelling. She never seemed to get any restful sleep any more.
Perhaps it was all the stress. Sometimes it took a real effort
to stay awake, especially in the afternoons. Today the problem
was particularly bad. She almost dropped off on the way to
the villa. Her head kept nodding forward and she had to shake
herself awake several times.

Perhaps it was time to buy a new bed.

Eduardo met her at the door, smiling broadly. 'There has been
a change of plan, Miss Carter. Signor Amato decided it was
not worth travelling to the city in this heat. He is in the length
pool at the moment. If you would like to go to the terrace, I
shall arrange some refreshments for you both.'

It was the last thing Katie wanted to hear. The temperature
must be up in the thirties. She dragged herself around the side
of the house. The pool was empty, but she saw Giovanni's
mark in wet footprints leading towards the pool house.
Walking around the water's edge, she remembered the last

time she had been here. The night of the party had been momentous. Now she was about to put herself in the way of temptation all over again.

Inside the pool house, Giovanni had already showered and towelled dry. He congratulated himself on deciding to miss that meeting in Milan. His absence from the villa might have given Carter Interiors the wrong impression. He was pretty sure that Katie would not come out in person. Not after she had run from him with such certainty.

He interrogated his reflection as he shaved. The first time he'd kissed Katie had been a mistake. He admitted that. Their lovemaking had been mutual pleasure, but then the scales had tipped against him. She wanted more than he was willing to give. That was why he had resisted every impulse to contact her since that night. She had run out on him. That was her choice.

He heard footsteps outside. Wiping away the last of the shaving foam he checked his appearance and went out to put on a polite show for the contractor.

Katie's head was pounding. With the sun almost right overhead any shadows were slender. She blinked. The dark was growing darker, the light brighter.

'Katie!'

She shut her eyes and then opened them wide. Giovanni was coming towards her from the pool house. She had no time to decide how she felt. His expression had gone from amazement to worry within a second.

'Katie? What is it? Are you all right?'

She could not answer. Suddenly, a wave of unbearable weakness almost knocked her off her feet. She reached out for him—but he was already there, supporting her gently as she slipped into unconsciousness.

The moment Giovanni strode into his villa with the unconscious Katie in his arms, his staff swung into action. They opened up the small guest suite and rang for the doctor. Reaching Katie's old room, Giovanni laid her gently on the bed. Her eyes opened while he was still bending over her.

'Katie? What is the matter?'

It must be serious. She saw concern in his eyes and heard anxiety in his voice, then ran out of time. Her stomach was swimming. Diving off the bed, she just made it into the suite's bathroom, where she was very sick into the sink. When she eventually returned, Giovanni was sitting on the edge of her bed, deep in conversation with Dr Vittorio. She tried to smile, without much success.

'I'm so sorry you've been troubled, Doctor. It's nothing. I don't think this heat agrees with me, that's all.'

The two men exchanged glances.

'Are you sure, Miss Carter?'

She stared at the doctor blankly. 'What else could it be? I was perfectly fine until I reached here. There hasn't been time for it to be a reaction to the water or anything. I only flew into the country this morning.'

'Are you pregnant?' Giovanni cut through all the concerned looks and came straight to the point.

'Giovanni!' The doctor was horrified at his lapse in tact.

Katie laughed, but soon stopped. Now she came to think about it, pregnancy might explain several things…

'It may have been badly put, Doctor, but there is a lot at stake here. Answer me, Katie?' Giovanni demanded in a dangerously quiet voice.

She burned with embarrassment. Raking over the embers of their passion like this, and in front of a witness, made her skin crawl.

'I—I don't know,' she whispered.

Giovanni raised his hands and let them drop to his sides. For a few glorious hours he had deluded himself. He had been wrong all along. Hard-working, discreet Katie Carter had never needed him for himself. As usual, it had been the money, privilege and position he could provide. The more he thought about it, the worse it became. If she *was* pregnant, it had happened suspiciously close to receiving that begging letter from her mother. Ensnaring a man through pregnancy was bad enough. To do it on behalf of a third party showed her to be as weak and silly as every other woman he had tangled with.

Katie moved her hand protectively across her stomach. 'A baby?' she murmured, feeling everything click into place. 'Perhaps that explains why I've been feeling so strange.'

'A simple test ought to confirm it, Katie,' Dr Vittorio was saying softly.

She looked at Giovanni with a blaze of spirit. She had spent weeks mourning the loss of him, when all the time she might have been carrying something equally precious within her.

Giovanni looked away. Sensing the atmosphere between them, Dr Vittorio sent him down to the kitchens. If Katie needed an examination, Nonna Bacchari's company was required. An unwilling father was not.

Later, the doctor went to find Giovanni. He found him sitting in the shade of an isolated summer house. After giving him the news, he retreated. Vittorio had dealt with the Amato family for long enough to know that Giovanni would need some time on his own.

That was true, but not for the reasons Vittorio imagined. The pain Giovanni felt was the agony of betrayal. It was indescribable. Katie had come back, but only to present him with the emotional blackmail of pregnancy. His instincts had been right all along. Now he knew why his father had spent so recklessly and lived so fast. There was no point in waiting for that one special woman. She didn't exist. If even Katie—clever, delightful, lovely Katie—could pull a trick like this, then there was no hope.

Part of him wanted to have her thrown out and abandoned like the scheming slut she was. Glowing with disappointment, he stood up and started on the long walk back to the small guest suite—but something slowed his steps. It was the memory of an unhappy child—absent parents, arguments and a life lived on the edge.

Giovanni vowed then and there that he was never going to let that happen to his child. Whatever it cost him.

'That was quick. Dr Vittorio said he was going to tell you to take a walk while you got used to the idea.' Katie lay in her shadowy room, watching the tall figure silhouetted on the threshold. He was watching her.

'I did.'

Crossing the room with heavy strides, he took a chair and sat down beside her bed. He was out of reach, but waves of anger flowed from him like static electricity. They burned Katie's happiness to ashes.

'I expected better of you,' he said coldly. 'I don't know which will be worse—being trapped into becoming a father or being the child of a one-night stand. What arrangements did you make at work before you left to come here?'

'They are expecting me back on the last working day in

July,' Katie said miserably. She had expected him to react to the news in the same way she had—overwhelmed at first, but then excited at the thought of their baby. Instead he was angry, as though the whole thing was her fault and hers alone.

'I had some holiday due,' she went on, wondering why he was not as pleased as she was. 'When I finish here, I plan to take a break in Florence.' She did not add that the thought of returning home while her mother was still there had been the spur for her first proper holiday in years.

'Good. Then you will stay here instead. My growing child must be protected from city air at all costs. Dr Vittorio says that an ultrasound scan should be able to give us meaningful information about the foetus within a month. After that, we can make a decision about the future.'

Katie could hardly take in what he was saying. It sounded so at odds with his simmering fury that she looked up at him uncertainly.

'So…you *do* want this baby as much as I do?'

He looked as though her question was too stupid for words.

'I doubt that I could, since a baby must have been central to your plans,' he said tersely. 'No, Katie. I need a son. You are young, strong, intelligent and—' he paused '—beautiful.'

He knew he should have smiled at this point, but the pain of her treachery was too acute.

'You will make a far better mother than some anonymous surrogate, which was Eduardo's latest suggestion for continuing the Amato line.'

'To think of it… Me—having a baby,' she whispered, smiling to herself. She was determined to be happy, whatever Giovanni's reaction. Now she would always have a part of him to cherish. 'I can hardly believe it…'

'You will have to get used to the idea.'

Katie pursed her lips. His scorn was bad enough, but it was sowing seeds of doubt in her mind. 'I hope I can manage,' she said uncertainly. 'Being a good mother is going to be difficult.'

'You should have thought of that earlier. But don't worry,' he went on crisply. 'Instinct coupled with all your other talents will see you through.'

'I didn't exactly have the best teacher when it came to parenthood.' Thinking of her own mother began to germinate Katie's fears. 'What am I going to do?'

Giovanni sighed. 'You will stay in this house until a scan can confirm that you are carrying my son. He must be born in Italy, of course—'

'*He?* What if it is a girl?'

'I need an heir,' he announced and then stood up. Without another word, he walked straight out of her room.

It was the clearest indication Katie could have that bearing a daughter was not an option. She lay down again and stared at the drawn curtains. Leafy shadows were playing over their thin summer-weight material. A branch of climbing rose had broken away from its support and was lolling across her balcony. She watched it dance without seeing anything.

If she had a son, her life would be over. He would be taken away from her. Her baby would be sucked into the aristocratic lifestyle that had made his father such a hard man. Giovanni must have a core of steel. How else could he make demands like these, using her unborn child as a bargaining counter? Things would be bad enough if he got his heir, but if she was found to be carrying a girl…Katie could hardly bear to think what might happen. She would lose Giovanni. And then she would have to return home to face her father's pain and her mother's horror, while she was kept alive only by the idea of Giovanni's baby growing inside her. All she would have to sustain her for the rest of her life was this single keepsake, a living memory of their one wonderful night together.

Unfamiliar tears welled up and rolled down her face. Katie prided herself on being able to cope with anything, but this was different. She could not bear it. Alone in a foreign country, scorned by the man she loved and tortured with sickness, it all became too much. She cried and cried until exhaustion overtook her.

When she woke the shadows had moved around. For a second she wondered what she was doing in bed during the day. Then she remembered.

'Congratulations, Katie.' Eduardo's voice came from somewhere near the foot of the bed. She struggled to sit up, at once confused and angry.

'Then Signor Amato has told everyone?'

Eduardo held up his hands with a smile. 'No—I am the only person he has trusted with the information so far. Although…Nonna and the kitchen staff have been in such high spirits this morning I doubt that his news is the total secret Signor Amato intends it to be. He will only make a formal announcement if the result of your scan is favourable.'

'You mean if I am expecting a son.'

Eduardo's smile became brittle 'After such a bad start, it is important to the count that his family name has a second chance to continue.'

'What does *that* mean?'

'The Contessa Lia died in—' Eduardo's eyes slid around the room, looking everywhere but at Katie. 'The late Contessa was never strong and she died in…distressing circumstances,' he finished somewhat secretively.

It all came back to that. Katie did not need Eduardo to finish his sentence. Giovanni's glamorous wife must have died without giving him the son he craved. That was why his family tree had been altered, to remove a painful memory. Now Katie was giving Giovanni a second chance, but all she could ever be to him was a runner-up in his race for immortality.

Anger began to make her feel better. Besides, she had to get up. People died in bed. That was what her father always said, immediately before recommending work as a cure for all ills. Not that it had done his heart any favours, but Katie was certainly not ready to follow the shadowy Contessa just yet. Cautiously, she swung her legs over the edge of the bed and stood up. It did not feel so bad, so she began searching for her shoes.

'I came to summon you to the dining room, Katie. Lunch is about to be served.' Eduardo checked his watch. 'The Count wishes you to be present. Even if you cannot face any food,' he added with a kind smile.

'Actually, I've just realised I'm absolutely starving!' Katie said in wonder. An hour before, sickness had convinced her that food would never touch her lips again. Now things were looking brighter. She dismissed Eduardo with her thanks and then took a quick shower. That therapy worked so well she felt almost human as she walked down to the summer dining hall.

The enormous table was already laid. When Katie had been shown to a seat, Giovanni dismissed the butler and got up to pour her some orange juice himself.

'Thank you, but perhaps I'd better stick to mineral water.'

'You are carrying a child, Katie—my child. You must learn to look after yourself properly.' He filled her glass to the brim.

She turned to plead with him, catching hold of his sleeve. 'Please don't be so angry. I never planned this—honestly. If you aren't happy about it, then I'm sorry. Just tell me what I can do,' Katie implored him.

He moved away from her and sat down. Seeing her agitation, he spoke. '*You* do not have to do anything, Katie. Everything is in hand. Bookings have been made, my diary has been rearranged, your office has been informed—'

'What?' Katie leapt to her feet, but his expression pushed her back down into her chair.

'Please calm down, Katie. My office merely informed your people that I had certain reservations about your designs and samples. They have been told that you will need to return here after your break in Florence to reassess my exacting requirements. The whole business is expected to take some weeks. That is the official line. In reality, of course, I have every confidence that your existing plans for my house will be exactly what I want. You will never leave the Villa Antico.'

Startled, Katie was relieved to see no trace of threat in his eyes. They were as watchful as ever, but that changed with her next words.

'All the same, Signor, I shall have to go back home to make sure everything is all right.'

'No. There is no need, Katie. Nobody is irreplaceable— except, of course, the mother of my son. For the next few weeks, all you need to do is relax, unwind and produce some new designs for the West Wing. Then, if necessary, it can be transformed into a state-of-the-art nursery section.'

Katie missed one of the implications of his words. She was too amazed at the other.

'But your father's "entertainment suite" is in the West Wing,' she whispered.

He turned on an inscrutable smile. 'Indeed, Katie, but I have never needed it and never will. If I have a son, it will be his nursery.'

'And what happens if I don't? What happens if my baby is a girl?'

Giovanni tore off a piece of bread to accompany his lunch. 'There is a fifty per cent chance it will not be. In any case, what can you do to influence the baby's sex? Nothing. So why spend the weeks until your scan worrying?'

'I'm being realistic.' Katie seized on some dimly remembered fact she had picked up somewhere. 'What happens if I miscarry? It's very common. Or the baby might not survive—'

He dropped his fork with a clatter. 'No.'

Katie shrank back. She had clearly touched a nerve and regretted it instantly. Contessa Lia's fate and that charity dinner on board the *Viola* began to form a horrible jigsaw of ideas in her mind.

'You…have had a child in the past?' She eased the words into the sunlit silence that enveloped them.

He picked up his fork again as though nothing had happened, but gave a brief nod. Nothing else was forthcoming. Eventually, after an agonising pause, Katie ventured a few more words.

'Will you tell me what happened?'

'No.'

The moment passed. With a sigh of regret, Katie picked up her cutlery and began her own salad. It was only when her mobile rang that they made eye contact again.

'Is it work?'

'No. It's my mother.' She sighed.

'I expect she will be delighted to learn of your pregnancy,' Giovanni said with a tinge of sarcasm.

'There's no way I'm telling her!' Katie said with a return of her old spirit. It helped her make an effort and smile into the phone. 'Hello, Mum. What can I do for you today?'

Her face fell as she listened to her mother's latest tale of woe. The neighbours weren't speaking to her, she had no money, her ex-husband wasn't willing to go on subsiding her—it was typical. So like her mother, so petty, so *normal*—

Katie felt totally abandoned. Giovanni was treating the baby she already loved as nothing more than a commodity. She wanted and needed support, but as usual all she got was orders and moans from every side... Suddenly it was all too much. Katie had had enough and burst into tears. Great unstoppable sobs poured out of her, drowning out everything else. Mrs Carter was so staggered she stopped speaking long enough for Katie to blurt out, 'I'm pregnant, Mum. I'm going to have a baby...'

Her mother's reaction was instant. 'Get rid of it. Get rid of it like I should have got rid of you. Children ruin your life. Look what has happened to me—'

It was like being kicked. All the air rushed out of Katie's lungs and she thought she would die. Her entire early life had been wasted trying to please her mother. She had been hurt and confused when nothing she ever did was good enough. Now she knew why. Her mother had resented her from the start. Katie had never been anything more than a mistake. It was a horror too great to put into words. Would Giovanni's anger affect her own poor, innocent little baby in the same way? The thought was too much to bear. With a terrified cry, Katie dropped her mobile and made a break for her suite.

A few minutes later she heard a knock at the door of her room.

'Go away!' She pushed her face deeper into her pillow.

There was a rattle as somebody tried to come in anyway. Katie had locked herself in, but seconds later she felt a presence beside her bed.

Giovanni had used the connecting doors that gave access

between the pairs of suites. The door was still shivering with the force he had used to throw it open. They glared at each other. His rage was uncomplicated. Hers was magnified through tears and fear.

On their first meeting, Katie had imagined him to be master of his emotions, only allowing others to see the image he wanted to project. The past few hours had swept all that away. Seizing a delicate Louis XVI chair from its place beside her tea table, he flung it towards the bedside and sat down on it. Katie lay still. She could practically see the fury engulfing him.

'I have just spoken to your mother,' he managed eventually.

'W-what did she say?'

'That's not important,' he answered quickly. 'What is important, is that I have informed her that we will marry if you are carrying my son.'

Katie frowned, puzzled. 'We will?'

'Of course.'

'Do I have a say?'

He gave a mirthless laugh. 'Surely you must have factored that into your calculations. Any Amato heir must be legitimate. That means marriage—but only if you are carrying my son. If not, then you will remain close so that I have access to my child, and you will be compensated accordingly instead. But only on one condition.' The look he was giving her changed. She guessed he was calculating how best to broach an unspeakable subject.

'Did my mother say the same thing to you that she said to me?' she asked slowly. 'Does she expect me to have an abortion if we don't marry?'

His normally calm features worked with suppressed anger.

'If you try to harm my baby in any way, Katie Carter, you will be thrown straight out of this house. You will be hurled back on to the tender mercies of your mother,' he growled, without bothering to hide his disgust.

Katie closed her eyes, flooded with relief. 'You need have no worries there, Signor Amato. Whatever sex our baby is, nothing could persuade me to do such a thing,' she said quietly. 'I would protect this little one with my life.'

His fists unclenched and his features lost their taut, dangerous look. Only when he regained his usual composure did he stand up to go.

'It does not sound as though your mother will be offering you much support, after all,' he sighed.

'That's my mum.' Katie tried to smile. 'It is as I told you, Signor Amato. Whatever talents she has, good parenting skills aren't among them.'

He stared at her as though gauging how best to answer.

'Your past is not as unique as you may think,' he said eventually, 'so perhaps we should both look on this as our chance to shine, Katie. We will show everyone how it is done.'

CHAPTER NINE

OVER the next few weeks Giovanni pushed himself harder than ever. He felt cheated, and it hurt. For a while he had connected with something really special in a woman. That feeling had not outlived their night together. She had abandoned him, only returning when she could use the missing part of his life as a bribe. So Giovanni threw himself into making the best of a bad situation. He toiled to consolidate the Amato fortune and made sure it would continue to grow. He re-drafted his will. The one thing he did *not* do was lay a single finger on Katie. They took their meals together, but only so that he could watch what she was eating.

The best books on pregnancy and child-care took the place of Dante and Jack Canfield on his reading schedule. It amused him that every source agreed that making love gently and in a restrained fashion should be perfectly safe.

The trouble was, Giovanni did not feel gentle and restrained. All he wanted was to relive that wild, exciting night of passion when their bodies and souls had soared, but it was too much of a risk. Katie had deceived him once already. His previous experience of women told him that she would do it again. For one brief moment he had been able to forget all the pressure, all his commitments and everything that had gone before. He wanted to take her to paradise again and again, to a place where she was Katie and he was Giovanni. He wanted to make up for all the times she had to rush grey-faced from his dining table, but his own pain and pride stopped him from bridging the chasm between them.

He had never known time pass so slowly.

The day of the scan arrived. Katie woke that morning with a different sick feeling. The nausea she suffered was easing, as peppermint tea and fresh ginger appeared regularly on the Villa Antico menu. It was apprehension at the thought of what the day might bring that made her queasy now.

Her appointment had been made in strictest secrecy. The staff were told that Giovanni would be flying to Milan on business, and Katie's decision to check on some fabric outlets was supposed to be a spur-of-the-moment idea. In fact it had been meticulously planned. The moment Giovanni brought his board meeting at Amato International to a close, he left to meet her at the clinic.

There was no question of queues and waiting rooms. They were ushered straight into a side room by a smiling young sonographer.

Katie's tummy was coated with gel. The operator apologised that it might be cold, but Katie did not notice. Her mind was filled with dread. She simply wanted everything to be over.

The probe rolled over and around the gentle swell of her belly. No bump was visible when she was wearing clothes, and now the unaccustomed sight of her pale, smooth skin transfixed Giovanni. He only stopped staring when the sonographer began to make cheerful noises.

'Everything seems perfect—all four chambers of the heart are visible and baby looks perfect for your date of the twenty-second of February—oh, and see this, Mama—baby is waving to you.'

Katie watched the flickering shape, wishing that Giovanni could take some pleasure in their achievement. This should be such a happy time for them both, but he had become so detached and silent.

And then the operator gasped.

'Ah, Signor—look—you have a son.'

Katie waited. Giovanni bent closer to the screen. There was a moment of absolute stillness. Then she heard him murmur something under his breath.

'Thank you, madam,' he said aloud to the operator. Then he put a hand on Katie's shoulder and shook it gently. 'Come along, Katie. We have things to discuss.'

He sounded almost pleased. She would have gasped, had her happiness not been tainted. She knew the future would be perfect for their son, but she would never feel Giovanni's love.

He had changed in an instant. Linking arms with Katie for the short walk to their car, he shortened his stride to fall in with hers. 'We must get home straight away. Eduardo has to be given the go-ahead for the arrangements. A date has already been pencilled in for the ceremony. All it needs is my confirmation.'

'Then we really are getting married?'

'There is no need to look so surprised, Katie. I told you my son must be legitimate.'

Her mind was not working properly. Ideas, hopes and fears all jumbled together. It was impossible to get a proper grip on anything. 'It's a lot to take in. I always dreamed that if I ever met Mr Right, his proposal would be a bit more…romantic, I suppose.'

'Very well—then, if you like, you can look through the

Amato collection as soon as we get home. You can choose yourself an engagement ring. Is that romantic enough for you?'

Katie had to nod, although the thought of wearing a second-hand ring chilled her blood.

'But first, we must send for my solicitor. He has drawn up the pre-nuptial agreement.'

The words weighed heavily in the air, snatching away any hint of romance.

They hardly spoke on the journey home. Katie stared out of the window, wrapped up in thoughts of her new, great responsibility to the house of Amato. Giovanni was silent, too, but for a different reason. His every movement now had new purpose and when they reached the villa he was firing off instructions before the helicopter's rotors had stopped turning. The staff were to be summoned to a meeting in the great hall, and Eduardo was sent down to the cellar in search of some Bollinger '92 to toast the occasion. Katie was sent up to rest until the time of the announcement. A few weeks earlier, she might have resented his order. Now it came as a relief. Besides, a strange change was creeping over her. For once in her life she was glad not to have to make decisions all the time. It felt relaxing and somehow *right* to let Giovanni shoulder some responsibility.

Despite Katie's new position in his household, Giovanni was not about to let Carter Interiors off the hook. Dr Vittorio thought it would be a good idea for Katie to keep her mind busy. Over the next few weeks the planned restyling of the Villa Antico went ahead, with her in charge. She was glad to get back into the routine of dealing with builders, decorators and samples. It was not as though she had anything else to do.

The new Contessa-in-waiting was attended night and day. Nothing was too much trouble. Nourishing, healthy meals were served to her at regular intervals. A car was put at her disposal. She had a beautiful suite, an estate to wander in, a choice of swimming pools—as her fiancé kept repeating, she could do what she liked, as long as it did not endanger his growing heir.

Her new life should have been wonderful—but there was something missing.

That something was Giovanni.

The wedding was arranged around her. Katie sat in her private drawing room like a queen as couturiers, florists, caterers and photographers arrived to spread out examples of their finest work before her. It was amazing. All she needed to do was ask and her smallest wish was granted.

She had been fitted for her wedding dress in a calico mock-up so she did not see the final result until her last fitting. That was on the day before the ceremony. The designers carried in a large cardboard box as though it contained a priceless treasure. It did. Katie instantly thought her wedding gown was far more beautiful than the most expensive design among the Contessa Lia's clothes.

The dress was made from finest raw silk, in a shade of cream that perfectly complemented her colouring. To distract eyes away from her midriff, it was cleverly cut and there was a matching stole lined with liquid silver silk. The skirt was embroidered with roses, violas and vines in the palest water-colour shades of silver, lavender and green. It was breathtaking. Katie still could not believe anything could be so beautiful when she was helped into it on the morning of her wedding. She wanted to look elegant rather than spectacular, and this was the dress. Her fervent hope was that Giovanni would realise how seriously she was prepared to treat her new role. He had practically accused her of tricking him into marriage. Katie knew she had a lot of ground to make up to regain his trust. To be his perfect bride on their perfect wedding day would be a start.

Her veil was held in place by a wreath of tiny mauve orchids flown in overnight from Singapore. In accordance with tradition, her bouquet was delivered on behalf of Giovanni. The florist had designed a matching work of art for her to carry. Sprays of the same beautiful little orchids joined fresh vine tendrils, trailing from a shower of cream roses. The effect was staggering.

Her parents and the entire staff of Carter Interiors were flown over to Italy in Giovanni's private jet for the ceremony. Katie's father was passed fit enough to escort her the short distance to the Amato family chapel, but when he saw her he was speechless. For a few precious seconds Katie allowed excitement to get the better of her. Everything was going exactly to plan. Everyone was telling her how lucky Giovanni was and how beautiful she looked. Surely her fiancé would be swept away by the romance of the day, too, and forget all his suspicions about her?

One look at Giovanni's expression when she reached the church dropped iced water on all her hopes. When he moved out from his seat to stand in the centre of the aisle, he turned his back on the altar to watch every step she made. He said nothing. When he bent to kiss her, Katie's reaction was to raise her hands and put them on his shoulders. The heat pulsed between them as their lips touched, but Giovanni did not indulge her for long. As they broke apart Katie let her hands slide down his arms in a sad gesture that was missed by the enormous congregation. They cooed with appreciation, but

Katie was dying inside. It was almost as though he had only planted a kiss on her to keep them happy—because it was expected of a bridegroom.

The ceremony passed Katie by in a blur. Formal portrait photographs had been made of the principal guests the previous evening, so only a few pictures were taken outside the chapel to record the event. Katie managed to smile, but she dared not look in Giovanni's direction. She could not risk seeing his expression. Here was a man who hated fuss and commotion, and now he was set right in the heart of it. Dignified in their own respective silences and scattered with a hailstorm of rice, confetti and tiny bags of sugared almonds, they walked to the grand marquee that had been set up outside the front of the villa. Swagged and lined in lilac, with flower arrangements to match Katie's bouquet, it was perfumed by crushed grass and a dozen different designer colognes. Katie visited each table, accepting kisses from all the male guests and good wishes from everyone. She smiled all day until her face froze into a mask of politeness. *Giovanni does not love me,* she thought. *All this is nothing more than window-dressing to him. He wants to save the honour of his family, nothing more.*

'Smile, Katie, or people will think you are not enjoying yourself.'

She looked up sharply at the low music of his voice. He was smiling—but not at her. Eduardo had brought him a message, and the relief on Giovanni's face was obvious.

'The helicopter is ready, Katie. It is time for you to begin your new life as Contessa, and for us to become officially man and wife.'

Giovanni had specifically asked that Katie did not change out of her wedding dress before they left on honeymoon. He

wanted the crew of the *Viola* to see her dressed as his
Contessa. His words made Katie feel even more like a symbol
than a living, breathing person. As soon as their helicopter set
down on the flight deck, he helped her out and together they
went over to the line of staff assembled to greet them. There
were more smiles and good wishes. Giovanni hurried the
moment along, checking his watch continually.

'The Contessa must be shown to her suite. It is time for her
rest,' he announced, and a maid led Katie through hushed corridors below deck into a panelled suite set with gold fittings.
With her flowers taken away to be preserved, Katie suddenly
felt very glad that Giovanni imposed such a strict routine on
her. Exhaustion had crept up unnoticed. As she undressed
and showered, her movements became slower and more
laboured. Despite half her mind being back at the reception,
wondering how her father was coping, she could hardly keep
her eyes open. The moment she slipped between the cool
cotton sheets, she fell fast asleep.

A maid woke her in time for a light supper packed with
goodness but sadly lacking in fat, sugar or salt. Katie thanked
her and tried to think of the good each healthy mouthful was
doing for her baby. When her tray was taken away, she was
left alone in a brand-new king-sized bed in a room decked
with flowers. The calm and luxury was beautiful. Everything
she could possibly need was in reach. It consisted of a gold
tasselled bell-pull and a bedside telephone complete with
printed directory of on-board facilities and international
dialling codes. Katie knew all she had to do was pull the cord
or lift the receiver to summon anything her heart desired—
with one exception. It looked as though her married life was
going to be as lonely as her single existence had been.

There was no pleasure in lounging alone. There were books

and magazines on interior design and Tuscan history. There was a television set with any number of stations. Her rooms on this luxury yacht were the last word in indulgence. Everything was marble, glass or gold plated, and it came with a perfect view over azure water and the sunlit coastline. All in all, her honeymoon had everything any woman could desire—except a husband.

It was not good enough. Katie decided to get dressed and go and find him. If nothing else, she had to thank him for being such a perfect host in the face of her mother's gushing approval. Joyce Carter had raved about everything, from the villa's monogrammed silver cutlery to its grass.

The *Viola* was even bigger than Katie remembered. She searched through every one of its public rooms before she found him. None of the salons were named, but as soon as she pushed open one set of doors Katie immediately knew she had found the music room. A full-sized grand piano took pride of place on a polished beech wood platform. Giovanni sat at the opposite end of the salon, beside an extensive sound system. He was lounging back in a large easy chair. His jacket had been lost at some point and his white shirtsleeves were turned back to expose the pale gold of his forearms. A brandy glass hung from the fingers of his right hand with a centimetre of tawny liquid in the bottom. His eyes were closed, but she knew he was not asleep.

Now she had found him, Katie did not quite know what to do. She entered the room and closed the door quietly behind her. His eyes opened, but he did not move.

'I'm sorry, Giovanni. I've been looking for you, but I did not mean to interrupt anything.'

'You apologise too much, Katie.'

Still he did not move. She had to do something, so she

walked towards him. Each squeak of the floorboards, every rustle of her skirt was magnified into a disturbance of his peace.

'I like the music you are playing. Is it Mozart?'

He nodded. 'It is a piece that is not heard as often as some of the others.' Taking a final sip of his cognac, he put down the glass.

'Would you like a drink? I had them put some fresh fruit juices in the fridge over there.'

'It sounds as though you were expecting me.' Katie tried to keep her voice light as she went over to a discreet serving area in one corner of the room.

'I thought you might take the opportunity to wander around your new territory.'

Katie poured herself a drink of grapefruit juice and added plenty of ice.

'I wouldn't presume to do anything of the sort. I was waiting for you to give me a guided tour.'

'Does that mean now?' He raised an eyebrow questioningly.

'It might be a bit more pleasant for the staff if they knew we were spending some time together, Giovanni, rather than apart.'

'A solitary lifestyle doesn't bother me. I prefer this to the noise and jangle of today's carnival.'

'That sounds a bit harsh.' She frowned, unable to bear criticism of a party that everyone else had enjoyed so much. 'It was good to see people having fun, especially the secretaries from Amato International. Don't you ever get lonely, keeping everyone at such a distance?'

He shook his head.

'I do,' she said heavily, staring at one of the enormous colour co-ordinated floral arrangements that flanked the speaker system. She didn't expect him to reply. When he did, it was a shock.

'Then come over here.'

Giovanni was still lounging comfortably in his armchair, but his eyes were alert. He watched her reaction intently. 'It is our honeymoon, Katie, after all.'

'I thought you had forgotten.'

He raised an eyebrow at the remark, and she bit her tongue.

'And I thought you had some sort of hidden agenda, Katie. You have been extremely quiet—ever since your return from England, in fact.'

Katie took a drink of her juice. Its bitter chill sent a barb straight down to her heart.

'I'm worried,' she confessed. 'And it isn't only the baby that is doing it—although goodness only knows how the poor little thing will cope with me as his mother. Work is my thing—not…not whatever it is mothers are supposed to do…' Katie floundered with the realisation she had no idea what was expected of her.

'We have an army of staff. You won't need to "cope" with anything. You will be in charge.' Giovanni spoke with quiet authority. 'But you hint that you have more concerns. All new mothers must have worries, but there is something else. I have seen it.'

Katie shut her eyes. She was making small circling movements with her hand, causing the ice in her drink to clink against the glass.

'It's only the same problem I've had since I was old enough to realise what was going on at home. Goodness knows how much Mum has persuaded Dad to spend on her for their stay at the Villa Antico—half a dozen changes of clothes, for a start. Since his operation, Dad's lost all his drive and he's always been a soft touch where Mum's concerned. He's been left sitting in the shade all day, while Mum's been hot on the trail of your friend Signor Balzone.'

'I know. I kept your father company for a while, when you were waltzing with Severino and the others. We had a long chat. He and I both prefer to talk than to dance, it seems.'

Katie sank into a chair on the opposite side of the salon from her new husband.

'Oh, no—don't say history is repeating itself,' she muttered. 'We have a phrase back in England: "If you want to know the wife, look at the mother." Well, it must be true. And to think—I've tried so hard to make sure I am different in every way. The hours I suffered, listening to her moaning about the way Dad hated partying. Now I am inflicting the same thing on you.'

'You knew what I was like when you agreed to marry me.'

She exhaled softly. 'It wasn't exactly a proper proposal, was it? This is nothing more than a marriage of convenience. The best thing for you would be if I disappeared off the face of the earth the moment your precious son is born.'

He sat up. 'No, Katie—you must *never* say that.'

Her eyes flew open at his tone.

For a few seconds his features worked, as though he was struggling with some inner demon. Then he spoke in a low, clear voice. 'My first wife died giving birth to our son. He was stillborn,' he added before she could ask for details.

'I see,' she said softly.

'No, you don't. There is much more to it than that. You spoke of history repeating itself, Katie.' He passed a hand over his face and she knew things were going to get worse. 'The night I saw you walking down the grand staircase in that green dress…'

Katie gasped. Eduardo's hoard of clothes could not be as secret as he thought.

'Oh, no…don't tell me I looked like your Contessa Lia…' her breath escaped in a low moan '…I couldn't bear it!'

For a moment his troubled expression became more thoughtful. 'No. You certainly did not look like her. You, Katie, were altogether more...desirable. It is just that I remember the night that my wife wore green—it was the night of our worst and most vicious argument.'

His eyes had been fixed on hers but now his dark lashes drew down a barrier.

Katie's mind worked feverishly. The gown Eduardo had lent her must have been put straight back in the closet after their quarrel. Giovanni *had* seen that unworn item and the argument had impaled its image on his mind. That was why he had been so transfixed. The diamonds must have been something Lia had worn. Katie thought of his glamorous last Contessa with an awful feeling of inadequacy. This was their world, not hers. She was an intruder here.

'No. That gown was thrown away later on my express orders.'

Katie had been about to confess, but on hearing that she changed her mind. She would simply have to live with her guilty conscience. Nothing would persuade her to get Eduardo into trouble.

'I only saw Lia's dress for an instant, but I hated it immediately. It stood for everything that was bad about our marriage. It was flashy—all show and no substance. When you appeared at the head of my staircase on the night of the estate party, Katie, for a split second I was about to send you back to change. Yet you looked so spectacular, no man could have resisted you.'

Certainly not me. He roused with the memory of it. Seeing the molten copper of her hair flowing over the glittering green gown that night had wiped all thoughts of Lia from his mind. That was until this instant. Her ghost now stood between them. It had to be exorcised, once and for all. To his surprise and relief, Katie had accepted the responsibilities of her position as well as the benefits. He wanted that to continue, but there was one last great test. He stood up and went over to the serving area in the corner. Taking a bottle of mineral water from the fridge, he broke its seal and poured a measure into a fresh glass.

'I don't feel spectacular at the moment.' Katie sighed. Somewhere, a clock chimed the hour and she automatically checked her watch. 'Right now, my father should be taking his medication. What happens if he forgets? I usually ring him with a reminder, but he told me not to bother while we're on honeymoon. What if he's relying on Mum? She'll be too busy to think of it. She's probably still making a fool of herself with one of your grand guests. I hope she doesn't embarrass you too much, Giovanni.'

'Don't worry about me,' he said brusquely. 'Go on—what else concerns you?'

'Isn't that enough?' She looked up at him hopelessly. 'The certainty that Mum will be off any day now and this time Dad will have no one at home to help him through it?'

'What about money?'

Her expression became guarded. 'Well, I suppose we should have discussed this a long time ago, but with Dr Vittorio being so in favour of me continuing to work now, I sort of assumed you'd be only too glad to see me go back to Carter Interiors once the baby was born.' She edged each word out, watching his face for clues about how he was taking her suggestion. When he did not immediately shoot it down in flames, she gathered a bit more courage. 'I *have* to work, Giovanni. Dad's council tax bill is over a hundred pounds a month, then there's the carer who pops in when I'm away, and regular bills for water, heat and light. It all comes out of my bank account and, as a self-employed person, I can't rely on any help with the costs. I'll have to get back in harness as soon as possible to cover it all.'

'I knew about your mother's bills,' he said grimly, 'but why have you never mentioned that you are supporting your father, too?'

She looked at him blankly. 'What else could I do? He is too ill to work, so it's my responsibility. Not that I think of it as any sort of burden, you understand,' she added.

Giovanni had been watching her closely. For weeks now he had been waiting for the requests to start—pay this, cover that—but they had never happened. Perhaps his earlier conviction that she was only after his money had been wrong. Perhaps it was time to put them both out of their misery.

Slowly, he went over and crouched beside her seat. Catching her hand, he squeezed it and looked deep into her eyes. 'Don't worry, Katie. Everything will be all right. I have already arranged to take care of all your mother's bills. Call it a wedding present from me. She will be told that this is the one and only time—'

'But Dad will still be left to bail her out in future.'

'No, he won't. I have something in mind to prevent him from backsliding.' A real smile began to warm Giovanni for the first time in weeks. 'Your father and I got on well today. I would have no objection to him coming to live at the Villa Antico. He could have his own suite, or a cottage in the grounds if he preferred. That way, you can keep a close eye on his health and welfare while I shall fortify him against your mother, if necessary. I have no patience with gold-diggers. Although for the truly generous in heart and spirit I have all the time in the world.'

Placing a kiss on her forehead, he tried to fill it with all the relief he felt. Distantly he was aware that they both put down their drinks and that Katie was searching for his lips. They kissed, and for long, luxurious minutes were suspended in their own personal heaven of sensations. It was Giovanni who was the first to manage his thoughts into some sort of order.

'Stop—Katie, just for a moment. If this is going to be a new beginning for us, then there is something more I must tell you about the Contessa Lia,' he said, and then words deserted him again. He wanted to be honest with his new wife, but the prospect of losing himself in her arms again after his self-imposed exile wiped every other thought from his mind.

'Talking about her can wait,' Katie murmured, leaning against him with a sigh.

CHAPTER TEN

GIOVANNI drew her closer. He had denied himself for weeks, aching for this moment. Now she was surrendering to him of her own accord. It was time. He took control and pulled her into another kiss so passionate that all inhibitions flew away. He had longed for this moment ever since she'd escaped from his bed. There could be no going back after this. He lifted her into his arms and carried her through the private quarters to his state bedroom. The place was in darkness. Large windows along one side gave a view of twinkling harbour lights across the bay. Everywhere else was velvet-black. The ship was silent and still.

For the first time in ages, Katie was alone with Giovanni in a bedroom. He laid her down on the bed and she sighed in anticipation. Through the darkness, the stark white of his shirt shimmered as it was thrown aside. Katie closed her eyes as she heard the quick quiet sounds of him shedding the rest of his clothes. Within seconds he was beside her, warm and insistent in the expectant darkness.

When they kissed, nothing seemed to matter any more. 'This is what I have been waiting for.' His voice was an urgent growl of primitive desire.

Katie felt a thrill of sexual excitement run right through her.

He held her close and there was no resistance as he covered her body and feasted on her lips. She gave herself up to wanton need, swept along on the crest of his overwhelming ardour.

His tongue probed between her lips, testing her and finding no resistance. When his mouth left hers to cover her throat with hungry kisses, she let out a long, low moan of pleasure. In response his hands glided over her body, her flimsy silk dress falling away as his hands sought her breasts.

Katie gasped as he cupped their growing fullness, his thumbs rolling over the hard, darkening points of her nipples. Instinctively she began to move her body against his, reacting to the tingling expectancy his fingers were teasing from her. Her hands began roaming his body, searching for a way to please him as he drove her up towards the stratosphere.

'No,' he warned her, 'I intend to make the most of this.'

He had waited so long to taste her again; nothing was going to make him hurry over the moment.

'Please,' she begged, 'I want you so badly, Giovanni…' Her voice ebbed away as he moulded his body to fit the curve and flare of hers. His palms moved over her shoulders, warm and assured. With each heartbeat Katie felt herself growing closer to him. Deep within her, a slow-burning fire was growing. He drank kisses from her now, savouring the taste of her lips, her tongue and her skin. She clawed at him, desperate for his attentions to go further. Digging her fingers into his hair she pulled her willing body up to meet his mouth. That was too much. Giovanni took back control, scooping up the dark luxuriance of her hair and cradling her head as his body moved in liquid accord with hers. As they kissed she felt the slow, sure movement of his hands on her skin. Passing down over her ribcage, he circled her hip, as her murmurs of delight became the birdsong of longing. When he parted the lips of her sex

she trembled in urgent anticipation. His caresses were irresistible, encouraging her writhing abandon as he caressed the
whole length of her, teasing the nub of her clitoris into swollen
arousal as he moved up, circled around and down, never lingering long enough to satisfy her, only heightening the sexual
tension that sang through the warm, dark night.

She was the first woman to offer herself to him so simply and
so wholeheartedly, he realised. His own arousal bucked against
the pressure of her body and he wondered with a hot twist of
pleasure how much longer he could resist total temptation.

She was ready: soft, warm and willing to bring him to
heights that she was already enjoying beneath his fingertips.
Pride and desire surged through him, fighting for supremacy.
In a few months' time this woman was going to give him the
greatest prize any man could wish for. He had proved that his
magnificent body combined libido with potency—and she was
the living proof of it. This moment deserved something special.

She released a gasp of protest as he left her, but it was only
for a second. His hands were already moving over her body
again as she opened her eyes to see what was happening. The
darkness had been pushed back a little by the soft glow of
dimmed lights. He drank in her naked beauty. Their first
couplings had taken place under the dark veil of night. Now
there was no hiding from him. She cried out and tried to cover
herself with her hands. Then she saw the effect that her body
was having on him. She looked up into his face, her eyes full
of eloquence.

'I want to see the body that is going to give me my son,'
he told her. 'I want to see what brought me such pleasure and
fulfilment over those few wonderful hours.'

There was no denying him. Any objections were stroked
away beneath his fingers. As he caressed the delicate folds of

her femininity all thoughts of embarrassment or shame evaporated. He appreciated each petal before moving deftly up to the heart and soul of her arousal. When he reached the rosebud of her clitoris, it was already beaded with dew. It swelled and blossomed beneath the pressure of his fingertip, making her cry out in helpless need. The sound triggered a primal urge in him. He lowered his head to taste her arousal.

The tip of his tongue teased her into a ferment of excitement. His hands moved upwards in long sweeping strokes, reaching for her breasts. The nipples were hard peaks, irresistible summits for his questing fingers. A similar bittersweet ache of tenderness was inspiring her. Sliding her legs up to encircle him, she felt the soft, dense spring of his hair against her inner thighs. In response, her muscles clenched and she sensed him pushing his body down hard against the bed, holding back his own urgency.

He could feel blood surging through every single vein in his body at once. The desire to enter her would not be denied. Where his tongue eased the path, his finger followed—slowly, carefully, gentling its way into her. She seized him with spasms of excitement, clenching and releasing in a way that raised a fine mist of sweat all over his body. It was incredible, but he forced himself to take things slowly. With infinite enjoyment he let her body set the pace. Each time she relaxed he probed a little deeper, until he could be sure that she could accommodate his towering need.

She called his name, over and over again, begging for release. Her body synchronised itself with his, moving with rhythmic thrusts that would soon draw them both to the peak of satisfaction. She was desperate for him, and him alone, in a way that no other woman had ever been. It delighted him and he could not get enough of it.

He rolled on to his side and let her nestle against him. The urge to sink straight into her was almost overwhelming. Eager for his body, she accepted him with a delight that swept away all restraint. Dipping smoothly into the waves of her passion, he gained release in a way that knew no limits. When he felt her muscles rippling over him in orgasm he unleashed his own body in waves of shuddering climax that wrenched a cry from deep within his soul.

Slowly, slowly, they drifted back to earth together.

'This is better than I ever dreamed it could be,' Katie murmured from within the protective circle of his arms. 'I have so longed for this moment... Oh, Giovanni, I wish I could be as happy as this for ever...'

She smiled into the deepening darkness. Her body and soul had been aching for years and now she knew why. All her life had been leading towards this moment. Loving Giovanni had taken her to a different planet. She moved the palm of her hand idly over her belly, back and forth. There was not a centimetre of her that he had not kissed and loved with a desire that made her head spin just to think about it. Then, as she drifted between sleeping and waking, a new, unknown feeling fluttered beneath her fingers.

'Giovanni! It's the baby!'

'What!' He was half out of bed before she managed to stop him.

'Don't worry—there's nothing wrong—I just felt him kick!'

'Where?' He flicked on a central light. Squinting against its glare, he strode back to the bed. All his concentration was on her naked body, but it was a different passion that consumed him now. 'Let me feel. Show me where he is.'

Katie lay on her back and took his hand, placing it low down on the gentle rise.

Within seconds his face was transformed with a smile. 'My Donatello is a lively little boy and no mistake. He is every inch his father's son.'

'Donatello?' The name catapulted Katie out of her trance. 'Where did *that* come from?'

'My great-uncle saved the Villa Antico and its estate from ruin. He raised me as his son during the frequent times when my father was…indisposed. I promised him on his deathbed that my son would bear his name.'

Katie could hardly argue with that, but she could not let it pass. 'You didn't think to tell me.'

'There was no need.'

She sat up, reaching for the sheet that had fallen unnoticed from his bed an age before. Covering herself up to her chin, she looked at him acutely.

'Does this mean I am to have no say in my son's life at all?'

Giovanni turned an impassive look on her.

'Donatello is first and foremost the Amato heir. Everything must be done to ensure his safety, security and well-being. That is why I act as I do. For example, Dr Vittorio has already booked you into the very best private hospital for your confinement.'

'*What?*'

'You will be moved there one week before the expected date of Donatello's arrival, unless of course there are indications that the transfer should be made sooner—'

'No—stop right there, Giovanni! You might have Donatello's life planned down to the last minute, but you can't do the same to me. I want to have him at home. I won't go into hospital. I *can't*!'

'But you must. It is the safest place for him to be born. How can you dream of bringing my son into the world in a place like the Villa Antico, which is so far from medical help?'

Katie began to panic. Surely no one could force her to do such a thing? Not after what had happened to her on the one and only occasion she had been admitted to hospital in the past. Her mother had abandoned her there. What would she lose this time? Her baby? Giovanni?

'There will be your friend Dr Vittorio on hand, Giovanni. Women have been giving birth for thousands of years without the benefit of hospitals. It's a perfectly natural occurrence. It isn't an illness!'

He was looking at her as though she was mad.

'I have my reasons, but they should not be allowed to trouble you, Katie. This is not a night for memories. It is an occasion to plan for Donatello's future.'

'And I have my own reasons,' Katie announced stubbornly.

He lay down beside her and stared up at the ceiling. *This is not the time or the place for explanations,* he thought. *But if not now, when? And if not here, where?*

The big black cloud threatening to engulf Katie rolled in. It had been hovering around for weeks, but Giovanni's unexpected show of emotion had brought it billowing right over her now like a shroud. In an instant she was seven years old again, held down by nurses and screaming for her mother, who had never come back...

'I can't go into hospital, Giovanni. I can't! Couldn't you just think about the idea of me giving birth at home, in the Villa Antico?' She edged around the subject as though treading on broken glass.

'Certainly not,' he said firmly.

And that was that.

Katie led a strange double life for the rest of the summer. While Giovanni was away at work she supervised a wonderful transformation of the Villa Antico. When he was in residence at the house, she lived according to his timetable. He had cancelled as many foreign engagements as he could, relying instead on conference calls and video links. He would not let Katie travel long distances, but that did not worry her. Work filled her days, and one or other of the limousines was always on hand for any short expeditions she might want to make. On the rare occasions Giovanni was not at his desk, he supervised her exercises in the pool or they caught up on their respective paperwork beneath the bowers of roses and vines on the pool terrace.

Before meeting Giovanni, Katie had been afraid that a close relationship would rob her of her independence. Marriage to an irresistible man, coupled with the seething hormones of pregnancy soon taught her a different lesson. Giovanni was accustomed to dabbling with intimacy, as and when he chose. Once Katie sailed away from the choppy waters of morning sickness, she could indulge her newly discovered passion. Giovanni was delighted. He was always ready to sweep her up to heaven, whenever she wanted. Things should have been perfect, and in a way they were. Katie had all the luxury she could handle. She was married to the world's best-looking billionaire and living in a house that was being refurbished to her exact designs. Her mother and father had declared a truce, although there was a cottage waiting for Mr Carter on the Antico estate, ready for when the inevitable happened.

Money was no longer a worry for Katie and she had the joy of making love to Giovanni.

But there lay the problem. She knew deep down it wasn't love—it was just sex. Bed with Giovanni was mind-blowing and brilliant every time, but Katie always felt something was missing. It was a long time before she could pin down her last remaining need. Then one day, between her daily aroma-therapy massage and her weekly shopping trip to Florence, she realised she would swap all the money and status and luxury for one simple thing.

More than all her other blessings put together, Katie wanted to be *loved*.

CHAPTER ELEVEN

As the year shrank away, Katie's baby grew. She watched Nonna Bacchari and her crew deal with the chestnut harvest, their old hands impervious to all the sea anemone spines. There was a bumper yield of grapes. Later, olives came in by the truckload. It was proving to be a fruitful year for the Antico estate.

And then, in late November, winter arrived. It was carried on alpine gales and they found every chink in clothing and houses. Little Donatello was the only one guaranteed never to feel it. Christmas came and Giovanni invited Katie's parents over for a month. Katie's mother complained about the cold, the isolation and the fact that she had to walk all the way through her dressing room to get to her marble *en suite* bathroom. The Carters returned to England after a single week. Katie could not help a sigh of relief.

The New Year roared in on a north-east wind. Glad of indoor work, the builders made good progress on the Villa Antico. With the nursery finished, they began stripping out the suite containing Lia's things.

'Are you quite sure of this, Giovanni?' Katie asked him a few weeks later over breakfast. The two dresses she'd borrowed had long ago been returned to their closets. They would now be auctioned along with everything else in the room, in aid of Giovanni's charity. It gave Katie a pang, but she had started discovering her own style rather than relying on Eduardo's secret supply of luxury. Besides, she never wanted to risk Giovanni recognising another gown again. 'You really do want to get rid of all Lia's clothes?'

'I have never been more certain of anything in my life.' He toyed with the silver spoon beside his coffee cup. 'And now, as my Contessa, Katie, you cannot possibly be expected to continue sleeping in the guest wing.'

At this, a tiny flicker of hope flared in Katie's heart.

'That is lovely, Giovanni. It will be a privilege to move into such a beautiful suite.' Her new rooms connected with his, but all she really wanted was the pleasure of sleeping with him every night, of being able to reach out and touch him whenever she wanted to…

'There isn't much urgency about that, of course. You will need time after Donatello's birth to regain your strength. I have discussed the matter with Dr Vittorio. Even if all goes well, it would be better to wait a few months before you conceive again.'

'We haven't had *this* baby yet!' She laughed, then realised that Giovanni was in deadly earnest.

'We won't be taking any chances.' His expression killed all the hopes she might have had of a happy-ever-after. 'Donatello cannot be an only child. That was part of my father's problem—he was never easy in his mind, knowing that all the family's hopes of succession rested on my survival. We will have to provide the house of Amato with at least one more son.'

He made them sound like machines for reproduction. In their short married life Katie had seen his mask of efficiency slip only once—when he had told her about Lia. All those years spent in offices full of job descriptions and timesheets had taken their toll on him. Katie put her hand to her stomach. At that moment Donatello gave a little wriggle and she felt her heart break all over again. This poor baby knew nothing about agendas or time-and-motion. She had a horrifying vision of Donatello's future. The fact that Giovanni had not bothered to tell her what was planned for the child growing inside her showed Katie where she came in the Amato pecking order. Right down at the bottom. She had no function here, other than to provide him with sons.

'And what if your next child happens to be a daughter?'

He motioned for another cappuccino. Stefano poured it out as his master gave a careless shrug. 'Then we will try again.'

Katie dropped her knife. Pushing back her plate with one hand and her chair with the other, she stood up.

'No. No, Giovanni, that cannot possibly be right.'

The butler rushed forward. 'Then shall I fetch you something else, Contessa?'

'No. My breakfast was fine, Stefano, thank you. It is my life that is all wrong.' Giovanni cleared his throat meaningfully. Katie did not care. 'Thank you again, Stefano. I think we can manage now.'

The butler bowed and reversed out of the room.

'Try not to lose your temper in front of the staff, Katie, it upsets them.' Giovanni took a sip of coffee.

'It needed to be said.'

'I don't see why. What is it about this life of yours that displeases you?' Giovanni looked genuinely puzzled. 'I provide you with the best of everything. All your plans for the villa are in place—now you have nothing to do but nourish my son and secure his future. By the way—I rang your consultant to request a viewing of the suite that has been set aside for you at the hospital. A visit in advance is bound to make you feel happier about going there for the birth.'

Katie's insides contracted with fear. A strangled cry escaped from her lips and she pushed her plate away. 'There you go again—forcing everything to fit your master plan. I can't even have my baby here at home, where I feel safe. You're going to have me bundled off, banished to hospital, where I can serve your purpose with no thought for my feelings at all!'

Throwing her chair aside, she stormed towards the door.

'Katie!' he called out but she did not stop.

'Come back.'

Katie took no notice. All he wanted to do was tie her down—to make her go into hospital—a place where only bad things happened. Her mother had not been there for her, and Giovanni would abandon her once he had his son, too.

She rushed out into the hall, reaching the front door and wrenching it open before anyone could do it for her. Her tears were burning fiercely, but now they froze in a blast of cold air.

Snow driven straight from the Apennines piled up in fluffy clouds of meringue against the north face of the villa. The staff had cleared a neat pathway out of the building, but it could not contain Katie's headlong dash. She blundered out on to the front doorstep, heading for the pure, clean snow of the forecourt. She wanted to stamp it, mark it, ruin its clean innocence in the same way her life had been trampled and spoiled by Giovanni Amato. In her blind rage she did not notice that freezing rain had glazed the snow with a surface as slippery as glass. Suddenly she was falling. Twisting to try and save herself, she crashed down heavily on to the hard, frozen gravel. There she lay, winded.

It was hard to catch her breath, accompanied by the sound of panicking staff and running footsteps. She began dragging herself up, her first thoughts for the baby. Then she sank down on to her knees. Just as Giovanni arrived to take control of the situation, a pain lodged itself in her spine.

'Stefano! Eduardo! One of you must ring for Dr Vittorio— quickly.' He stepped out of the villa and bent to help her to her feet.

'There's no need. It's just my back. The baby is fine. He's OK.' Katie pulled herself out of his grasp and tried to scramble up unaided. Her head was ringing and there was such an ache where she had wrenched herself.

'But how are *you*?'

She looked at him sharply. There was real concern in his eyes and it echoed through his voice.

'I'm fine, too.' Katie smiled, although she had a cold, terrifying feeling that she might not be. Something about the pain refused to die but, if she told him, he would send her away to hospital.

'Then we can manage by ourselves now. Thanks, everybody.' Giovanni nodded to the staff members who had followed them outside. 'Go and ask one of the girls to make sure the Contessa's room is ready, would you?'

Giovanni and Katie were left alone outside the great old house. She looked up at the north face of the villa. From here, it still looked bleak and bare, but inside she had transformed it into a home. This was the place where she wanted her baby to be born.

'You need not bother yourself on my account, Giovanni.'

'That was a nasty fall. I shall not be happy until you have been examined properly.'

She looked into his face and was shocked out of her anger. For once, she could believe him. His eyes had softened to dove-grey and were questioning her silently.

'I was trying to get away,' she said, shamefaced.

'There was no need, Katie.'

'There was every need. Giovanni, you dictate my every waking moment. You're going to take my son away and feed him into some hellish system that turns out aristocrats to order and, worst of all, you are going to make me go into hospital.'

Giovanni hesitated. He could see that her anger was a front. More than anything else, she was frightened. His mind still reeling from the effect of seeing her crumpled in the snow like a broken flower, he was taking some time to come to terms with his feelings. Seeing her reduced to this affected him deeply.

This entire situation was his fault. At the start, his body had wanted her too desperately to avoid those first fateful misunderstandings. Later, his mind had taken over, keen to salvage something from the situation. Their marriage of convenience had been the logical outcome. Now, when he least expected it, his heart was taking control.

'There are two good reasons why I must insist on a hospital confinement, Katie. You and Donatello.' He watched her face. She looked as shocked as he felt at his sudden compassion.

'People die there.'

'People sometimes die because they cannot get there in time.' He put his arm around her. She responded to his cautious gesture by leaning against him, gingerly at first, but then with more conviction. It felt good. He smoothed her hair. 'You will see when we visit next week—there is nothing to be afraid of. It will be the best place.'

'Not for me,' she said miserably. A tear dripped onto the snow, then another, harsh shards on his conscience. 'My mother took me there to have my tonsils out and while I was away she left home. It was an excuse to walk out of my life until I could be of some use to her. What am I going to lose this time? My baby?' *And you,* she added with a silent cry of yearning. *Although how can I lose you when I have never really had you?*

'Dr Vittorio is out on a call, Signor.' Eduardo appeared at the front door. 'He should be here within the hour.'

'Good. Then I will take the Contessa to her room. We are not to be disturbed under any circumstances, Eduardo, until the doctor arrives.'

He lifted Katie into his arms and started towards the house. 'There is something I must tell you, Katie,' he murmured as he made his way carefully up the stairs. 'I'm sorry, but it will not be an easy confession for me to make. Or for you to hear…'

CHAPTER TWELVE

SHE had to be told the truth, and it had to come from him. Giovanni took a deep breath and then another, but they reached her suite and still he had not managed to say anything. Then, because he sensed that she was about to start questioning his silence, he laid out his private nightmare as they reached her bedroom.

'Katie, the fact is that I killed my first wife. It was my fault Lia died.'

He felt her body go rigid beneath his hands.

'You don't mean that.'

'How I wish I didn't,' he muttered, laying her gently down on the bed.

'But…how?' There was a nervous suspicion in her beautiful eyes and her voice could barely rise above a whisper. Giovanni could feel waves of apprehension flowing from her. There was no going back now. She would have to hear the whole sad story.

'Lia left me, only returning when she discovered I had made her pregnant. She lived a frivolous lifestyle and she didn't want the responsibility that came with being a contessa. Yet, when she realised that producing an Amato heir would provide better benefits, Lia decided to stick with the devil she knew. The problem was, she never looked after herself. She was too interested in fashion to put on enough weight. Her diet consisted mainly of probiotic drinks and cereal bars. Nothing the doctor or I could say would persuade her to eat properly. Lia and I were living in a flat at the top of the Amato building at the time. She wanted to be close to the shops and I was so overwhelmed with work it was easier to live at the office. Lia's parents didn't think it was a grand enough place to welcome our child. They wanted the baby to be born in their palazzo. My father was no help. He sided with them. He was in residence here at the time. The Villa Antico was the best place for him, away from all the temptations of town.'

His shoulders had been drooping, centimetre by centimetre. Katie watched, biting her lip. She said nothing, because there was nothing to say.

'In the end, I became so sick and tired of all the arguments I let them all get on with it. Everything was taken out of my hands. A team of specialist nursery designers flew in from California. They produced a suite at the palazzo that outshone anything in the glossy magazines. Lia had her portrait painted. The baby's name was put down for public school. A flock of Norland Nannies was ready to take care of him from the moment he was born. The only thing missing was a sense of reality.'

'And common sense, by the sound of it,' Katie said quietly.

Giovanni raked a hand through his hair—a movement of frustration and anguish. Katie put tentative fingers on his shoulder. He looked back at her. Now she understood the reason for the torment that clouded those grey eyes.

'I should have stood my ground and insisted that Lia's safety and the life of my child were the only things that mattered. My pride did not allow it. When complications set in, she was stranded at her parents' house, out in the middle of nowhere. Lia was never strong. She did not survive the journey to hospital—which was delayed because her parents could not decide whether she should be transported in a *public* ambulance,' he finished bitterly.

'And your baby was stillborn?' Katie asked gently.

It was a long time before he replied. The old wounds were obviously as raw as ever and he was looking straight into them. 'He could never have survived in that condition…' He sighed. 'The doctors told me that these things happen, but we all knew it was because Lia did not eat enough of the right food or look after herself properly.'

Katie vowed from that instant never to complain again about the way he policed her meals.

'That is why I must beg you to reconsider, Katie. I cannot bear to think of the same thing happening again.' He took both her hands in his, enclosing them in warmth. His voice became more urgent, speeding up as though time was running out for them both. 'Over the past few months something has changed between us—but I didn't allow myself to admit it until a moment ago. I have been totally blind. When I saw you looking so helpless and afraid just now I realised I had driven you too far. I can't lose you now, Katie, because the truth is that I—' He stopped. Words deserted him, and for long moments all he could do was look at her. Eventually, when he had not managed to say the one thing that would change everything between them for ever, he had to think of something to switch the focus back on to her.

'Why didn't you tell me about your fear of hospitals?' He levelled a serious gaze at her.

'I—I thought it might go away…and then—and then I realised that you had less reason than my mother did to be there for me… Once you had Donatello, you would both be out of the door and I would lose you…' She ran out of words, too. All she could do was stare at him, willing him to hurry up and say something more. Her pain had started to advance and she was beginning to feel very strange.

'I have been doing some thinking, too, Katie. Our marriage should not be like this. I admit responsibility for my own actions, but it must be said my father was not an ideal role model. All his life he loved unwisely, and too often. I have been so determined not to repeat his mistakes, I may have gone too far in the opposite direction. Yes, I need an heir. It is such a powerful desire within me that I almost lost sight of the blessing that was already within my reach…Katie, what is it?'

'N-nothing. Just one of those practice contractions you're always telling me to expect…' Her words ended with a groan. She curled forward, trying to make the pain small. It did not work.

Giovanni's arm tightened around her shoulders.

'Don't worry. It will be fine.'

He slid into control mode. Encircling her with one arm, he reached over to the bedside telephone. As he was ringing for help, Katie creased again. Abandoning the call, Giovanni laid her back against the pillows. He started telling her that help was on its way, but she could no longer register anything beyond the pain that would not let her go.

It went on and on. People came in and out of her room, bringing linen and newspapers and reports that Security had just admitted the doctor's car. Nonna Bacchari brought ice for her lips. Life whirled around her, but for Katie it was reduced to the circle of Giovanni's arms.

'Oh…Giovanni…this wasn't supposed to happen. I've done something terrible to Donatello, and you don't even love me…' she managed weakly.

He held her close to him, feeling that at last he could pour the words into her. 'Work and the past have stopped me admitting it to myself until now, Katie, but I *do* love you. Now I realise how wrong I have been, not revealing how I truly felt. Please forgive me, Katie… Let me love you. Let me keep you safe here, for ever…'

The doctor burst in on a ripple of cold air. Once his examination was complete, he took Giovanni aside. Katie was left in the care of Nonna Bacchari. The old lady sponged her face and gave her more ice to suck.

'Oh, but it is such a shame you will not be able to get to the hospital.' Nonna shook her head and sniffed in disappointment. 'You should not have to give birth at home. I thought my generation would be the last to have their kids like this.'

'What about all your grandchildren and great-grandchildren? Wouldn't you prefer them to be born on Antico land?' Katie was struggling to keep awake between pains, and wondered if this was a bad sign.

'No, no, no!' The old woman cackled with laughter. 'This is the twenty-first century, Contessa. Hospitals are palaces of leisure today. Everything is to hand, there is no washing up…any woman who has the chance of going there seizes it with both hands. It is the only place we can get any rest. Ah, but then things are different for you. We are here to do everything for our Contessa.'

Nonna stopped laughing so abruptly that Katie knew something was seriously wrong. She opened her eyes as Giovanni slipped his arms around her again. His expression was so tortured that in an instant Katie knew her own agony and fear no longer mattered. She would make any sacrifice now, just to stop his pain.

'I—I've changed my mind, Giovanni,' she said quickly

before he could get a word in. 'This feels as if it's going to be a lot tougher than I thought. I—I should really like to go to hospital, please,' she finished with a gasp.

'After what happened to you there the last time? After all you have said?'

She nodded. At that moment the look of total relief on Giovanni's face was worth everything to her. Going into hospital would be unbearable, but it would ease his torture and she had to think of little Donatello, too. He was being catapulted into life early, and kilometres away from any specialist help. Her future meant nothing, if anything happened to him.

'Are you sure, Katie?' Giovanni asked softly, but they both knew it was only a formality.

She nodded. 'You wanted Lia to go to hospital and she wouldn't, and you have been blaming yourself ever since. You aren't going to lose a second son, Giovanni. I won't let it happen. You *must* take me to hospital.'

He was silent until the next contraction rushed between them. Her grip tightened on his hand like a tourniquet. Covering her fingers with his own, he hung on. 'Don't worry, Katie. I am *never* going to run out on you. You won't have to suffer anything alone, ever again. I shall be here for you, every minute of every day.'

'Of course you will,' she said flatly, as another shot of pain smashed her into fragments. Giovanni gathered her up, pressing his face against hers as she gasped and tried to catch her breath.

'Believe it,' he murmured. 'Believe me, Katie. I will not leave you. I love you. I need you.'

The terror ebbed away. Katie came to her senses and realised she had been crushing his hand again. Releasing her death grip, she watched the blood flow back into his whitened fingers. It saved her having to look him in the face as she spoke again.

'I understand. And now—all that matters is Donatello. And you.' She put out a hand to touch his face. Then the pain rose up again like an instrument of torture. It dragged her back, crushing her like a rag doll. When it passed she took a long time to gather her strength again.

'Listen to me,' she whispered quickly, afraid that the pain might silence her forever next time. 'What happened before— it is not going to happen again. Donatello is well fed and strong. He takes after you. He will be all right.'

Giovanni bent down to rest his brow against hers. 'But what about you?'

His forehead felt ice-cold. She realised it must be because her own was burning-hot. She tried to smile. Giovanni could not even pretend to do the same. She was so pale that even her lips were losing their colour. Instinctively he reached out and grabbed her hand again. It was cold and grey. He brought it to his lips and kissed her fingers. The bitter taste of salt lingered.

'I can't bear to think of you going through the same thing all over again.' She tried to moisten her lips with her tongue, but now Nonna had taken the ice cubes away it was too much of an effort. 'Perhaps…perhaps we could make a start for the hospital?'

'I shall ring for an ambulance.' Dr Vittorio was fumbling for his mobile, but Giovanni was already on his feet and heading for the doorway to summon help.

'Eduardo! Go and tell the men to get the helicopter ready— right now. I shall fly you myself,' he called back to Katie before he was engulfed by a hubbub of preparations.

'Dr Vittorio?' Katie's voice rose weakly from the bed.

'Yes, Contessa?' He leaned close to catch her voice.

'Giovanni is under a lot of pressure.' She tried a smile, hoping that he would return it. 'Make sure he does not fly as fast as he drives, would you?'

Giovanni carried Katie out to the helicopter. Placing her gently inside, he could hardly bear to let her go, but time was slipping away. He kissed her longingly and then hauled himself into the pilot's seat.

'I want to go on holding you, my love, to keep some contact with you, but I need both hands. I have to concentrate on the controls. It's the weather—'

Sleet was driving horizontally into the windscreen.

'It doesn't matter, Giovanni. Talk to me. I shall hold on to your voice.'

'You're going to be all right,' he said, concentrating on the switches and blinking lights of the display before him.

'Yes—as long as you are more careful in the air than you are on the roads.' Katie managed another smile for Dr Vittorio, who was crouched beside her. He did not return it.

'If we are going to reach the hospital, we should leave immediately, Giovanni.'

Katie shut her eyes. The doctor must mean the weather was closing in.

Giovanni was not so sure.

Staying conscious was becoming more and more of a struggle. The pain was a rolling wave now. It dragged Katie back and forth in a cold dark sea, sometimes allowing her to come up for a gasp of air but more often submerging her in its depths. Suddenly her face was spattered with real drops of water. The air she was almost too weak to breathe was forced into her lungs by a tremendous down-draught. There was noise—

clatter, confusion and rattling as she was jostled and jolted out of the helicopter and onto a stretcher. She tried to open her eyes, but it was raining hard. And there were too many voices—loud, angry sounds…

'There. Didn't I say I would never leave you?' Giovanni was speaking quickly into her ear. 'I shall be with you for every second of the time. Don't leave me, Katie. I love you too much.'

'And I love you, too.' She tried to put her fingers out to touch the face she could no longer see. As she did so her hand was grabbed and stabbed, but there was no time to ask why. Everything—the cold, the pain—was already beginning to ebb away. Katie sighed. She did not care. The only thing that mattered was one voice and those three words.

'I love you!'

He said it again. He was saying it to her. The last thing Katie remembered before it all slid away was: *He means it. He really wants me. I am going to get over this, if it kills me…*

Things got very confusing after that. Katie drifted in and out of consciousness. There was so much noise—electronic pulses and alarms, the clatter of steel on steel, the sound of people moving about. They all hovered around the edge of her awareness, but nothing matched Giovanni's warm reassurances.

Whatever the medical team was doing continued in near silence. Then a waterfall of gurgling snuffles formed itself into a wail so tiny that it was drowned by congratulations. Giovanni was kissing her and saying all over again how much he loved her. Katie heaved a huge sigh of relief. Everything was going to be all right for Giovanni this time. He had his little Donatello, safe and sound. Her job was done.

She could let go and sleep.

* * *

Some time later, Dr Vittorio spotted Giovanni out in one of the hospital's floodlit quadrangles. He was leaning back against a wall, eyes closed, his face raised to the fine freezing drizzle. The doctor pushed open a door and called out from the warm security of the corridor. 'Giovanni? What on earth are you doing out there? You should be inside.'

'I came out for a few seconds to use my mobile while Katie was asleep. Everyone must be given the news.'

'I hope you aren't thinking of flying yourself home tonight?'

He shook his head. Pulling out his phone, he tapped in the villa's private number. 'I won't be parted from Katie now. I am going to ask Eduardo to arrange some transport home for you, Doctor. I was too distracted to think of it earlier.' He gave an exhausted sigh.

'Look, I'm sorry, Giovanni. Mistakes happen, but—' Vittorio looked away and clicked his tongue.

'I'm not bothered about all that now.' Giovanni's attention snapped back to more pressing matters as his call was answered.

'Eduardo? Yes, yes, I shall tell you everything in a moment, but right now I need you to bring my car…'

The first time Katie woke, it was still dark. A bird was singing not far away. She moved her head. The curtains of her room were closed, but harsh electric light was poking in through a gap. It must be either very early in the morning or late in the afternoon. Gradually, she came to realise that nothing was hurting any more. Revelling in the memory of Donatello's little cry, she relished the absence of pain for a minute. Then in the darkness she began trying things out—wiggling her toes, putting an experimental hand on her tummy…

Her small movements alerted the nurse on duty in her room. The woman rustled forward with a smile.

'Shall I call your husband? He is only just downstairs, with your daughter.'

Katie frowned. This must be a case of mistaken identity. 'My daughter? No, that can't be right—Giovanni has a son, Donatello. Where is he?'

'There, there.' The nurse expertly silenced Katie with a thermometer under her tongue. 'It's nothing to worry about, dear. Baby swallowed a bit of fluid, so they want to give her a thorough examination. Your husband was torn between staying with you and going with her, but I told him to go. You were supposed to sleep for hours yet,' she finished briskly, checking Katie's temperature and marking it on a chart.

Too weak to argue, Katie settled back into her pillows and closed her eyes. The nurse must have mixed her up with some other mother. Giovanni Amato had his son and heir, so nothing else should matter.

But something mattered very much. Her new family was nowhere to be seen. Aching with sadness, Katie came to a terrible conclusion. Everything was running true to form, after all. The aristocratic machine had absorbed her little Donatello. His proud father was probably already supervising the re-gilding of his family tree, back at the Villa Antico.

As Katie slipped into sleep again, her lashes thickened with tears.

'I told you we would be back before the Contessa woke,' Matron sang out, waking her.

Katie opened her eyes and gasped as Giovanni entered her room. He was drilling one of his killer looks into the nurses who accompanied him. A small white bundle was cradled in his arms.

'You should know better than to hand a baby over as though it is nothing more than a caterpillar in a cocoon, Matron,' he was saying. 'This is *my* child, after all!' He scowled as all the staff fluttered away.

Carrying the baby as though it was an unexploded bomb, Giovanni lowered himself carefully on to the chair beside Katie's bed.

'What *do* they think I pay them for?' he said in disgust.

Katie's voice cut quietly through his indignation. 'I thought you had gone.'

His beautiful eyes still contained all the power he had used to rally her during those long dark hours. She gazed back, breathless with the realisation that she had been wrong. He had not deserted her. His promises had all been true. It hadn't been a dream.

'I told you I would never leave you, and an Amato always keeps his word,' he said with quiet conviction. 'Now, Katie, we have things to do. We must choose a name.' He settled the little bundle in her arms and pulled a small book from the pocket of his jacket. Katie was too busy staring down in wonder at their new arrival to notice in detail what he was doing. The baby was so tiny, with perfect little features set in a face not much larger than a clementine. Only a little over nine months ago she had fallen for Giovanni so completely she had felt her heart would never have room for anyone else. Now she knew differently.

She looked up into the face of the only man she would ever love, as though waking from a dream.

'You chose Donatello and that is fine by me since you want to honour your great-uncle. Once you had explained the reason for your choice, I understood.'

He laughed and it was so natural and unforced that Katie reached out and touched him in delight.

'Giovanni, you are the last person in the world I would have imagined with stubble, designer or otherwise.'

He put up a hand to cover hers, pressing it to his cheek. 'And whose fault is that? It feels as though I have not been home for days.'

'Oh, I know the feeling,' Katie sighed.

Her eyes were drawn back to the little bundle in her arms. It was wrapped tightly in a white shawl. With nervous fingers, she pulled back a fold. A tiny mottled fist protested against the touch of fresh air. Catching hold of the identity tag attached to the baby's wrist, she read it out loud.

'"Baby Amato. Weight 2.41 kilograms. Female." Oh, my goodness—Giovanni?'

She looked at the baby even more carefully. Now she came to think about it, that tiny face certainly looked very feminine. Baby Amato had a mouth like a rosebud and the dark lashes fringing her tightly closed eyes were even longer than her father's.

Looking up, Katie gazed at him with growing wonder.

'You needed a boy so badly, but she's a girl. And yet you are still here?'

'I shall have that sonographer shot at dawn,' he said, laughing softly. 'Oh, Katie—how many times do I have to I promise I will never leave you?'

'Please keep saying it. I can't hear it enough. You have been saying a lot of other things, too.' She smiled at him, almost shyly. 'I seem to remember something about…love?'

He could not tear his gaze away from his wife and their new arrival. 'Throughout my entire adult life, Katie, I have told only one woman that I love her. And that is you, Signora Katie Amato.' Putting aside the book he leaned over and kissed her tenderly. The moment was only broken when the baby between them began to stir. Katie smiled dreamily into Giovanni's mist-grey eyes. He was looking at her with a new honesty and it was gentle. All her fantasies about a future in Giovanni's arms, surrounded by flocks of his children, swam back into her mind.

'Do you think,' she said carelessly, as she began investigating their precious bundle, 'that you might also consider saying it to a *Luisa* Amato, for example?'

He tried it out for himself a few times, then nodded. 'Luisa. Yes, I think that would be perfect for our beautiful baby. Who is almost as beautiful as you,' he finished in a murmur as he kissed her again.

THE ROYAL HOUSE OF NIROLI

...International affairs, seduction and passion guaranteed

Volume 1 – July 2007
The Future King's Pregnant Mistress by Penny Jordan

Volume 2 – August 2007
Surgeon Prince, Ordinary Wife by Melanie Milburne

Volume 3 – September 2007
Bought by the Billionaire Prince by Carol Marinelli

Volume 4 – October 2007
The Tycoon's Princess Bride by Natasha Oakley

8 volumes in all to collect!

THE ROYAL HOUSE OF NIROLI

*...International affairs, seduction
and passion guaranteed*

VOLUME TWO

Surgeon Prince, Ordinary Wife
by Melanie Milburne

His first heir excluded from the throne, the King
summons his family to his side… Then discovers the
grandson he thought was dead is still very much alive!

Alessandro Fierezza was snatched as a baby and
held for ransom by ruthless Vialli bandits. But when
brilliant Australian surgeon Dr Alex Hunter arrives on
Niroli to help the ailing king, rumours abound that he
is the missing prince!

Amelia Vialli is a dedicated nurse, helping the poor
of Niroli, but has had to live with the stigma of being
a Vialli bandit all her life. When Dr Hunter appears,
Amelia falls instantly under his spell, unaware of the
intrigue that surrounds him.

*But when Alex discovers the truth, he's torn between duty
to the ruling family he's never known and his passion for an
ordinary woman who can never be his queen…*

Available 3rd August 2007

4 FREE

BOOKS AND A SURPRISE GIFT!

We would like to take this opportunity to thank you for reading this Mills & Boon® book by offering you the chance to take FOUR more specially selected titles from the Modern™ series absolutely FREE! We're also making this offer to introduce you to the benefits of the Mills & Boon® Reader Service™—

- ★ **FREE home delivery**
- ★ **FREE gifts and competitions**
- ★ **FREE monthly Newsletter**
- ★ **Exclusive Reader Service offers**
- ★ **Books available before they're in the shops**

Accepting these FREE books and gift places you under no obligation to buy, you may cancel at any time, even after receiving your free shipment. Simply complete your details below and return the entire page to the address below. You don't even need a stamp!

YES! Please send me 4 free Modern books and a surprise gift. I understand that unless you hear from me, I will receive 6 superb new titles every month for just £2.89 each, postage and packing free. I am under no obligation to purchase any books and may cancel my subscription at any time. The free books and gift will be mine to keep in any case.

P7ZED

Ms/Mrs/Miss/Mr ....Initials ....

BLOCK CAPITALS PLEASE

Surname ....

Address ....

....

....Postcode..

Send this whole page to:
UK: FREEPOST CN8I, Croydon, CR9 3WZ